Annie Annie

Annie Annie

MOLLY CONE

Illustrated by Marvin Friedman

HOUGHTON MIFFLIN COMPANY BOSTON

Other Books by MOLLY CONE

Mishmash

Mishmash and the Sauerkraut Mystery

Mishmash and the Substitute Teacher

Mishmash and Uncle Looey

A Promise Is a Promise

The Real Dream

Reeney

The Trouble with Toby

Crazy Mary

Hurry Henrietta

The Other Side of the Fence

Contents

Annie Annie

1 Annie Annie

THE telephone rang. Annie lay across her bed and listened. She let it ring twice before she answered. It would only be Migs.

"Annie?"

She could picture Migs hanging on the telephone across the street. Everybody used the same telephone in Migs' family. Migs' mother didn't believe in children having their own telephones. She didn't believe in kids choosing their own clothes, or even in regular allowances. Migs never had to decide anything for herself, thought Annie, a little bitterly.

"Did your mother say you can go to the Fair?" Migs always spoke in a hurried voice over the telephone. Probably because her mother never let her talk more than three minutes. That was the rule in their house. Three minutes.

"Oh," said Annie. "I didn't ask her."

"You didn't ask her!"

Annie shrugged. "She'd just say it was up to me. I'm supposed to decide things like that myself."

"Well, you're lucky. I had to beg and beg. My

mother doesn't believe in girls going to public places alone," Migs said piously.

"You wouldn't be alone," Annie said in a practical tone. "Five thousand, two hundred and thirty-one people went to the Fair yesterday — that's what it said in the newspaper."

Uncomfortably, Annie recalled that her father was always saying you have to think before you believe everything you read in the newspapers. *Think.* She made a face. It was her father's favorite word. "Of course, I didn't count them myself!" she added.

Migs giggled as if Annie had said something that was supposed to be funny.

"Naturally, I didn't tell my mother about the boys," Migs giggled again.

Annie sat up. "What boys? You didn't tell me about any boys, either."

"Didn't I?" Migs was pretending, thought Annie. She could always tell when Migs was pretending. "Well, I guess I just forgot," Migs said hastily. "Tom Jacobsen, and maybe Art Healy."

"Oh," said Annie. "Tom Jacobsen." And the pain of just saying the name muffled her voice. Tom Jacobsen had never even bothered to say hello to her. "Well, have a good time," she said, and hung up.

Tom Jacobsen. She lay back. Once at a slumber party, every girl was supposed to say right out loud who her secret love was. In dutiful honesty, Annie had said — Tom Jacobsen.

The telephone rang again. She listened to two rings and waited until she heard a third and a fourth before she picked up the telephone.

"We must have been cut off," said Migs imperturbably.

"Not really," said Annie.

But Migs went right on, eagerly. "He wants to meet us there." Her voice was full of her excitement.

"Us?" It wasn't even a question.

"Well, not exactly. As a matter of fact, I didn't tell him we'd planned to go together."

"Well, thanks," said Annie.

"I wasn't really sure you could go," said Migs hurriedly.

"You're right," said Annie. "I can't."

Migs gave a little gasp. "But you just said — "

"I've just made up my mind," Annie said. "I can't go." And she hung up again.

She got off the bed, stuck her feet into her shoes and went downstairs.

Her younger brother, Howard, was sitting in the living room talking to an older boy. It was Awful Jones. Annie walked right past, pretending not to see them.

Migs' mother wouldn't let Migs even *talk* to Awful Jones.

Annie's mother came in from outside and paused to look in on her way upstairs.

"Hi, Mom," said Howard.

He said offhandedly to his friend, "This is my mother," and said to his mother — "His name is Awful. Awful Jones."

"Hello, Awful," Mrs. Lee said pleasantly.

Awful didn't answer.

"Say hello to my mother," Howard prompted.

Awful mumbled, "Lo."

"He doesn't talk to adults," Howard explained matter-of-factly. "He'll only talk to kids."

Annie guessed it didn't surprise her mother. What kids did never seemed surprising to her mother. Annie listened to her mother go up the stairs, then she went on into the kitchen.

Everyone said that Howard took after his mother, Annie reflected. They both yelled at the top of their voices when they were excited. They both laughed loudly. They both had round faces and liked to watch football games over television. Annie didn't care much about watching football games. She didn't even care especially that no one had ever said she was like her mother. The truth was, no one had ever said she was like her father either.

She stood in the kitchen and looked at the breakfast dishes still on the kitchen table. She began to take the clean dishes out of the dishwasher and stack the dirty ones in. Through the window, she could see her father out on a lawn chair reading. Her father often fell asleep when he was getting a haircut or watching television, but he never fell asleep when he was reading.

Like Regina, thought Annie. When she was home

from college, Regina was always too busy to do anything around the house, but she was never too busy to
go to the library.

Regina took after their father, thought Annie.
Slowly she began to set the table for lunch.

She made some tuna fish sandwiches and set them
daintily on a flowered plate in the center of the table.
She laid out paper napkins and a bowl of potato chips.

"Lunch is ready!" she called.

No one answered. Her father went right on reading.
Her mother went on doing whatever she was doing.
Her brother went on talking.

Annie poured herself a glass of milk, helped herself
to a sandwich from the plateful and began to eat. There
wasn't any particular rule around their house about
lunch. If you were hungry, you ate — any old time.

It was different at Migs' house. Everybody ate at a
regular time. They all had to get up at a certain time,
too. And no one, not Migs or her three little sisters, or
Robert, her twin, or her older brother, Peter, was
allowed to say anything at the table that had anything
to do with stomachs, or feet, or blood, or war, or
money. That was certainly different, thought Annie.

The front door slammed. "What's to eat?" asked
Howard. His eyes were like a squirrel's, thought Annie;
he even looked as if he stored nuts in his cheeks. She
watched him pick up a sandwich, inspect its filling, and
place it back on the plate again. She looked at his hands.
Everybody at Migs' house had to wash with soap before
they even sat down to the table for lunch.

"Hey, Mom!" Howard yelled at the ceiling. "We got tuna fish sandwiches!"

Upstairs a door closed and his mother came down the stairs. Outside, Mr. Lee marked his place in his book and put it down. Annie took another bite of her sandwich, and pretended she was enjoying it.

"Delicious!" Mrs. Lee said enthusiastically as she helped herself.

It didn't mean anything, Annie told herself. Her mother was just naturally enthusiastic. She even nodded with an air of exuberance like a stout elm in the wind.

Annie's father was more of a stunty scrub pine. He squeezed down into his chair without hitching it back. He rubbed his elbow thoughtfully before he picked up a sandwich. He took a bite. "Regina always put celery in with the tuna," he said, and squinted thoughtfully at it.

Annie had forgotten about the celery.

"The mail came," said her mother. She meant a letter from Regina. Mr. Lee looked up.

"She's staying another week in Ghana. And she says she's finally met someone she wants to marry."

"An African!?" Howard almost exploded.

An odd feeling of apprehension filled Annie. She wondered what Migs would say to Gina's coming home married to an African.

Her father took the letter and read it for himself. "She doesn't really say," he said in his dry voice.

Involuntarily, Annie saw a handsome black face under a white turban. He would be handsome; Regina's boyfriends were always handsome.

"Will he have a ring in his nose?" Howard began to squirm in his chair. Howard was almost fat. When he grew excited about anything at all he wriggled and squirmed as if everything he wore was too tight for him.

"Naturally," Annie said quickly. "And he'll have saucer earlobes and tattoos all over his forehead and wear a flowered skirt."

Her father smiled. It was only the slightest lift of the corners of his mouth, but it was a smile.

"Zowie!" Howard nearly fell off his chair. "A brother-in-law with a ring in his nose!"

Her father laughed, a real laugh. Her mother was smiling.

"I wonder how he blows his nose!" Howard said. "With a ring in it, I mean."

Annie put her sandwich down and pushed back her chair. "I think — " she said loudly and disapprovingly — "when kids are brought up to say anything at the table there is something wrong with their bringing up!"

"Annie, Annie — " her mother said, and Annie could see she was trying hard not to laugh.

Her father simply stared at her.

Annie whirled about. "I'm going to the Fair!" she shouted at them, and pounded out of the house.

2 "My Mother Won't Let Me"

ROBERT OPENED the door at Annie's ring. Though he and Migs were twins, they didn't look much alike.

"You going with Migs?" He grinned at her.

Annie stared back at him. She didn't like Robert much — he always smelled of chest rub.

"It's Annie," Robert yelled over his shoulder. "For Migs."

"You can tell her to wait out on the porch," his mother said.

"I'll be ready in a minute," Migs called out to her.

Annie sat on the porch and waited. It was a large porch that went the full length of the front of the house. There were two bicycles neatly standing against the railing. There was a porch swing, and three pots of geraniums and a baby stroller. Everything was very neat. Even the mat had been swept. Migs' mother was a good housekeeper. She *liked* cleaning house. The kids in Migs' family were supposed to be polite and do their lessons. That's all they had to do. They had to *ask* before they invited company. Annie wondered what it would be like to be Migs instead of Annie. Involuntarily she made a face. She wouldn't like Robert for a twin brother!

Annie bent her head and tried to hear what they were doing in the house. The big front window was the living room window. Sounds of voices were coming from there.

Migs' mother always made them stop whatever they were doing once a day to say Hail Mary with her. Usually they said their Hail Marys after dinner, Annie reflected, but she guessed that today they were saying the rosary after lunch instead.

Annie listened, trying to catch the sound of the words. She counted three Hail Marys. Migs' mother would be counting off the beads on the rosary as they all recited. That's what the rosary was for. Sometimes Migs' mother let Annie sit in the living room with them while they said the rosary, but Annie was just as pleased not to be invited in today, she told herself stoutly.

She sat on Migs' porch and stared at her own house across the street. It wasn't at all like Migs' house. There was no wide porch. There were no windows downstairs that looked out on the street; the living room faced the back garden. It was a reverse plan house. And Annie made a face.

It seemed to her, sometimes, that everything about their family was reverse plan. Her mother, for instance, going down to her office every day, and her father doing a lot of his work at home. It had never occurred to Annie that there was anything unusual about that, not until it seemed funny to Migs.

"You mean your father can go into the kitchen and cook anything he wants to!" Migs talked as if a man in a kitchen was against the law or something.

"Well, why shouldn't he?" Annie had demanded.

Migs had laughed. "It just seems funny — I mean a man *cooking*."

Migs' father had never wiped a dish in his whole life, that's what Migs had said.

"My mother and father are very *liberal*," Annie had told her with careful dignity. It was a word they used in their house a lot, but it hadn't impressed Migs at all. Migs hadn't even known what she meant. She hadn't cared either. One thing about Migs — she was sure that being Migs was the only way in the whole world to be.

Suddenly Annie wished she felt like that. She wished she could be like Migs. She wished her house was like Migs' house, and her family more like Migs' family, and that they all said Hail Mary together every single day!

The door behind her opened and clicked shut again.

"Come on, before my mother forgets she said I could go!" said Migs, running down the steps. They walked quickly up the block.

"My mother and father have to go out tonight," Migs giggled. "They're going to a dance. They've been practicing in the kitchen all week."

"My mother and father go dancing quite a lot," Annie said.

Migs looked surprised. "But your mother is *taller* than your father."

"Well?"

"They must look sort of funny — dancing together."

"My mother is too intelligent to let a few inches bother her," Annie said stiffly.

"Well, my mother isn't!" Migs said flatly.

Annie grinned.

Migs regarded her critically. "Who do you take after? Your mother or your father?"

Annie felt her chin growing warm. "I don't have to take after either of them."

"Yes you do." Migs was positive. "My brother, Peter, says you'll be either a little taller or a little shorter than either of them. What you won't be is right in the middle. It depends on who you take after — your father or your mother."

"I'm not anything like either of them," Annie said too loudly and looked away.

Migs' hand grabbed at Annie's elbow. "Here comes that Awful Jones!" She grimaced.

He was slowly coming toward them. A guitar hung from a shoulder strap. He didn't raise his head and he didn't even notice them.

"What's he coming down this way for?" Migs said. "He lives way over on the other side of the school."

"He's probably coming to see Howard," Annie said uncomfortably. "He was over talking to Howard this morning."

"Howard? Your brother?"

"Of course, my brother."

"But your brother is only a little kid. He's only eleven. Awful is almost as old as my brother, Peter —

and he's sixteen! You mean he comes around to talk to *Howard!*"

Annie shook Migs' arm away. "He never talks to adults. Just to kids."

Migs laughed. "He does the craziest things. My mother says she's seen him sitting around downtown. Just sitting on a curb as if there were no traffic or anything. Once my mother asked him why he didn't go home where he belonged, and he didn't even answer."

Annie said again — "He just talks to kids."

"Well, it doesn't make any sense to me!" said Migs, and turned suddenly and crossed to the other side of the street.

Annie kept right on going. "Hello, Awful!" she said loudly as she passed him.

He didn't answer.

Migs continued on, down her side of the street, without crossing over again. They walked that way, on opposite sides, all the way to the bus stop. Then they got on together and sat in the same seat.

"Look who's in the back of the bus," Migs whispered.

"Who?" said Annie, turning around.

Migs poked at her. "Tom Jacobsen. Do you think he's seen us?" She kept her head carefully faced forward.

"I don't know," said Annie.

The bus started up, stopped at the next corner, started, stopped, and finally got into the arterial going to the Fairgrounds.

Another bus passed them. *Ride the Skyride at the*

Fair. The advertising banner was pasted on the back end.

Migs shuddered. "I wouldn't. Not for anything." And then she jabbed at Annie with her elbow. "What's he doing now," she said in a whisper. "Is he looking over here? Do you think he sees us?"

Deliberately Annie turned around and looked back.

"Hi!" called Tom, and the boy beside him grinned at her.

"Hi," she said coolly, in return, and turned around again.

"He knows you're here," Annie reported. And turned to stare out the window.

Tom got off with them. The other boy was right behind him. He reminded Annie of Robert.

"Hey!" Tom said to them — "the Skyride opens to-day."

"I know it," said Annie, while Migs said — "Really?" as if she'd never heard of it before.

"They're going to be giving away free scones at the flour exhibit," Tom's friend said.

"Oh I love scones!" said Migs.

"I don't," said Annie.

"Well, come on, then!" Robert shoved Migs forward.

"I'm coming," said Migs with a giggle.

"No thank you," said Annie, and she walked quickly in the other direction. She ducked into the art exhibit, and walked slowly through the gallery and out the back entrance. She looked around awhile and then went on the Skyride. She rode around and around all by herself, enjoying it until she looked down and saw Migs and Tom Jacobsen strolling along together below.

They caught sight of her and waved and hollered.

"Take the next ride!" she shouted.

But Migs shook her head and Tom Jacobsen cupped his hands to his mouth and yelled importantly — "We can't! Migs' mother won't let her!" — while Migs went on chewing into a caramel apple with modest little kittenish bites.

The truth was Annie didn't feel much like riding anymore either but she went around again before she came to that conclusion. It wasn't the sort of thing you could change your mind about in the middle.

When she came to the stop, a boy was standing there.

"Hey!" he called at her. "You having fun?"

"No," she said.

He laughed as if he thought what she said was funny.

"You going around again?"

"Why not?" she said. She stayed on and when she got off he wasn't there.

She stumbled out and grimaced at herself. Migs would have known what to say. Migs did anything she wanted and when she didn't want to do something, she said — "My mother won't let me."

"You want to buy a balloon," a boy said, plunging them into her face.

Annie said experimentally, "My mother won't let me," and then laughed at the expression on his face.

She looked then at the watch on her wrist, and with-

out thinking about it turned toward home. She was supposed to have sense enough to come home at a reasonable time. Annie sighed. Migs' mother always told her exactly when to come home. She didn't expect Migs to have any sense at all.

Awful Jones was sitting on Howard's bed. He was just sitting there, doing nothing, with the door wide open.

"My brother's not home," Annie said pointedly, pausing in the doorway.

He raised his head, noted her, and looked down again.

"I don't know when he'll be home!" she said more loudly.

He looked at her curiously a moment, and must have decided she was a kid, like himself —

"Do you think your mom and dad would care if I bunked in with Howard for just a night or two?"

She shrugged. "I don't know. They'd probably say it was up to Howard. It's his room. Once my sister Regina kept an alligator in her room for three weeks and they didn't say anything."

He looked at her startled, and then grinned.

"They don't care much about things like that," Annie felt she had to explain. She looked at him a moment. He wasn't dirty, and his hair was combed. Migs' mother didn't think boys should have long hair. "What do you want to come here for anyway?"

"I can't stay home."

"Why not?"

He made a face. "My parents."

"What's wrong with your parents?" Annie asked politely.

"We had an argument over my guitar."

"What's the matter, don't they want you to have it?"

"Sure, they bought it for me."

"Well?"

"They want me to take lessons."

"You mean you have it and you don't want to learn to play it?"

"Sure I want to learn to play it! But that doesn't have anything to do with taking lessons!"

Annie twitched her shoulders.

"My dad says the only way to learn to play is to take lessons. When he was a kid *he* took lessons. My mother says, I *have* to take lessons because if I don't I'll make all kinds of mistakes."

Annie looked at him doubtfully.

"I told them that's the way I want to learn — by making mistakes. I like to listen to other kids, or records, then try to play my own way. That's the way I like to learn new things. Doing it my own way."

"Oh," said Annie. "I see."

"My parents don't," Awful said glumly. "They can't see it at all. All my dad keeps saying is that I have no ambition. He's always talking about ambition." Awful made an inverted U of his mouth. "What's ambition for?"

Annie thought about it. "I guess it's supposed to be for money."

"That's it!" Awful said. "That's it exactly! My dad thinks being ambitious is the answer to everything. Every single thing in the world!"

Annie made a face too. "With my father it's education. He thinks all the answers to everything are already in books."

Awful laughed hoarsely. "Well, they aren't. If they were, all anybody'd have to do was go to the library!"

He raised his hands and let them fall on his knees. "It's no use talking to them. It's not any use at all!"

"I see what you mean," Annie said, and thoughtfully she went out and closed the door behind her.

3 "Doing It My Own Way"

"You mean you're going to live with somebody else?" Migs asked her in a small shocked voice.

"It's a live-in job!" said Annie. "I have to live there if I'm going to take the job."

"My mother wouldn't let me," said Migs.

"How do you know? You haven't even asked her!"

"And I'm not going to ask her!"

"Well, I'm not going to *ask* my mother either," Annie said.

Migs said flatly — "You don't have to ask her."

"That's right," Annie said, as if it were great to have parents who didn't really care what you did.

"Anyway, they'll only say it is up to me. They'll probably be relieved not to have to bother with me all summer."

"That's what my mother comes right out and says about sending me to camp. She says it will be a plain relief not to have me around!"

"That's different," said Annie. "Your mother is *making* you go to camp."

"That's so," said Migs, but the subtlety of the difference had somehow escaped her.

"Honestly, Migs, sometimes I think you don't *think* at all."

Migs looked thoughtfully out of the window. "What will you do if your mother says no?"

Annie looked at the card she had removed from the supermarket bulletin board. She read it again. *School girl wanted. Good Christian home. Live in.* They hadn't asked her if she were Christian, she reflected. She would have had to tell them that her mother and father had never gone to any church.

Mrs. Sigby had only asked her if she had ever opened the Bible. She had said yes, unhesitatingly. It had been the truth. She had opened it once to insert a four-leaf clover for pressing.

She couldn't remember ever opening it again though. Until the moment Mrs. Sigby asked her, she had forgotten all about that four-leaf clover. It had suddenly seemed very lucky.

"Well, just *suppose* she says no," Migs persisted.

Annie thought about it. "They might object a little bit," she said. If they really objected, she told herself, she'd just have to tell Mrs. Sigby that her mother wouldn't let her. "My mother won't let me," she would say, and she smiled broadly.

Migs flopped back on her bed and stared at the ceiling. "Do you believe in Fate?"

Annie remembered how she had been walking past the supermarket and had happened, just happened, to stop and look at the community bulletin board there. "Sometimes I do!"

"I do too," said Migs. She turned her head and added cautiously — "but don't tell my mother."

"I won't," said Annie.

Someone had put up an ad offering to pay for used comic books; there was a garage for rent and a reducing machine like new for sale. A girl named Nancy had advertised that she was available to take care of pets while the owner was on a trip, or walk dogs . . .

"Do you think anyone would actually pay money for baby-sitting dogs?" Annie asked Migs.

"Not to me, they won't!" Migs said promptly.

"It doesn't appeal to me either," said Annie. She sighed. "It probably was Fate that I was the first one to answer Mrs. Sigby's ad."

"How do you know you were the first one?"

"Mrs. Sigby said so. I took it right off the bulletin board and got on the bus and went over there. I told her I'd let her know right away if I was going to take the job."

"Are you really going to?"

Annie stared at the picture of Jesus over Migs' bed. He had long hair. "I haven't decided," she said.

"I'm thinking of getting a job," Annie said at dinner. Her father was drinking his coffee, leaning on the table, his arm in front of him.

"I'm thinking of getting a gerbil," Howard said loudly. He had a book in his lap; he hadn't even noticed she'd been talking.

"A what?" said her father. He hadn't noticed either, thought Annie.

"What in Heaven's name is a gerbil?" her mother asked.

"It looks a little like a teensy tiny chipmunk without the bushy tail," said Howard. He lifted the book from his knees and read aloud: "*Mouselike burrowing rodent of Africa and Asia having a long tail and long hind limbs enabling it to leap like a jerboa . . .*"

"They're about the size of a hamster and they don't smell," Howard said. "Anyway the girl said they don't smell, and they're supposed to make excellent pets."

They hadn't even *heard* her, Annie thought.

"Remember when Regina ordered an alligator from the Sears Roebuck catalog?" said Mr. Lee. He chuckled hoarsely. "She kept it in a tank in her room."

"An alligator!" shouted Howard.

"You were just a baby," said Mrs. Lee. "You wouldn't remember."

"It grew to be about a foot long," Mr. Lee said, "and when it was out of the tank it snapped at people."

"We finally had to give it to the zoo," Mrs. Lee said. "It was Gina's first pet. She was heartbroken."

Annie didn't remember that. "Over an *alligator?*"

"Why not over an alligator?" said Howard. "I can remember you bawling your eyes out once over a kitten."

"That's different," said Annie with a sniff. "Kittens are human."

Her father looked at her in surprise.

Annie flushed. "I mean the same as human."

"I'm going to keep them in a cage in my room," Howard said.

"It's getting pretty crowded up there, isn't it?" Annie said.

Howard shrugged. "Awful won't care. I've already asked him."

"Asked him!" said Annie.

Their father was looking from one to the other in puzzlement.

"He means Awful Jones," she said to her parents.

"Who is Awful Jones?" their father asked.

"He's staying overnight with me," Howard said.

"You mean he's upstairs *now?*" Mr. Lee said.

"He brought some peanut butter sandwiches," Howard explained.

"Peanut butter sandwiches!" said Mrs. Lee.

"He likes peanut butter sandwiches," Howard said patiently. "I told him that was okay — he didn't have to eat dinner with us if he didn't want to."

"Of course, he doesn't have to if he doesn't want to," their father said, and Annie looked at him closely. Sometimes it was pretty difficult to tell whether their father meant exactly what he said. She guessed he didn't because, suddenly, her mother laughed.

"Tell him he's invited, anyway," Mrs. Lee said.

"He's going to help me make a cage for my gerbils," Howard said. "He's never made anything like that before."

Mr. Lee took his weight off his elbows and said dryly, "Naturally, that makes him eminently qualified."

But it made sense to Annie. Naturally, Awful wanted to figure out how to do it his own way.

"You could go to the library," Mrs. Lee suggested. "They must have plans for all kinds of cages at the library."

Annie snorted. She couldn't help it. It was a loud, incredulous snort. She stood up, and stared purposefully out of the room.

"Annie?" her mother called after her as if she had just remembered that Annie had started to say something but she wasn't quite sure what.

But Annie's mind was already made up. She didn't even bother to reply.

4   A Matter of Responsibility

SHE PACKED her bag. Underclothes, brush and comb. Soap and toothbrush. She folded her best dress and put it in, then on second thought took it out again and hung it back in the closet. She guessed she wouldn't need a party dress to help Mrs. Sigby in the kitchen. Annie chose two cotton skirts and three blouses, a pair of pajamas, and her library book. She would be coming home on Sunday. That was her day off, Mrs. Sigby said, and part of Saturday too.

She awoke suddenly in the middle of the night remembering she had gone to bed without brushing her teeth. Her toothbrush was in the bag she had already packed. Sleepily, she arose, unpacked some of the stuff, found her toothbrush, and went down the hall to the bathroom. Someone had left on a light downstairs, she noticed, and she went down to turn it off.

Awful was there in the kitchen, eating his sandwich. He was sitting at the kitchen table with peanut butter on his mouth, and his hands busy with something on the table.

"The cage," he said. "I'm trying to figure out how to make a cage for Howard's gerbils."

"In the middle of the night!"

"It was just an idea," he said modestly. "When I get an idea I like to get right at it. Like sometimes I hear a tune in my sleep and I like to get up and try it. No matter what time it is." He grimaced. "My parents say that's crazy."

"Once Regina got up in the middle of the night to bake a pie," Annie said. "But she fell asleep while it was baking."

"Were your folks mad?"

Annie glanced up at the ceiling. Her parents' room was directly above. "They never got mad at anything Regina did. My father came down and took it out of the oven himself and we all had it for breakfast."

"Pie!"

It was exactly the tone of voice Migs had used when Annie had told her about it the next day.

"Migs' mother doesn't let anyone in their house even eat between meals," Annie said. She opened the refrigerator door.

"Would you like a piece of cake?" She faced him squarely. "My father made it."

He wiped the peanut butter off his face. "My father wouldn't know how to fry an egg!"

"I know," she said carefully. "Migs' mother doesn't even let her father into the kitchen." She cut a slice for Awful. "It has a gooseberry filling," she added a little apologetically. "My mother and father like things like gooseberries."

Awful nodded. "And alligators."

Annie said, "Personally, I don't think I'm any crazier about gerbils than I am about alligators."

He looked at her thoughtfully.

"I like kittens better," she said. "And cats and dogs and goldfish." There was a bowl filled with goldfish in Migs' living room.

"Say, do you think your mother or father would mind if I use these barbecue sticks?"

"You going to barbecue now!"

"To make one side of the cage," he said patiently. "I found them outside on the porch."

"They've probably already been used for weiners and marshmallows and things," Annie said.

Awful took a bite of the cake.

"Howard never gets up in the middle of the night," Annie said. She contemplated the contents of the refrigerator. She might as well eat, she had to brush her teeth anyway. "Would you care for some milk?"

He shook his head. "I figure that I can make a pretty good cage out of just an old box, maybe. I could turn it on its side and put these sticks over the open end for bars."

Annie looked at the sticks doubtfully. "Wouldn't the gerbils be able to squeeze through?"

Awful scratched his nose.

"Maybe you could use a wire screen or something like that."

There was a sound from above. A squeak was followed by a thump.

"Annie!" — that was her mother's loud voice. "Is that you?"

There was a slight pause. "Well, don't forget to shut the refrigerator door when you come up!" There was another squeak as her mother got back into bed.

Annie shut the refrigerator door.

Awful was looking at her curiously.

"They don't care," she said dully, and went back upstairs to bed.

She dumped everything out of her overnight bag and packed it again. This time she put her toothbrush on top.

She came downstairs the next morning carrying her overnight bag.

"I'm going to take a job," she said clearly. "At Mrs. Sigby's. It's a live-in job. Helping."

Neither her mother nor her father said anything at all. They just stared at her. She wondered if they had heard.

"It's over on Fifteenth Street. They have a married daughter who doesn't live home anymore. They have a vegetable garden and two apple trees. Mr. Sigby used to run a grocery store but he doesn't work anymore. Mrs. Sigby is very nice. Her canned vegetables won a blue ribbon at the Fair last year."

"Canned vegetables?" said Mr. Lee.

But her mother said calmly — "That sounds like a very good idea."

Annie looked at her suspiciously.

"I mean it." Her mother was not looking at Annie but at Annie's father.

"Lots of girls Annie's age take summer jobs. I'm sure it will do her a world of good."

Annie glowered.

"I think it will be good for Annie to have the responsibility."

"I won't have any responsibility," Annie said loudly. "Mr. and Mrs. Sigby said they'd *tell* me what to do."

But the point was seemingly lost on her parents. They went on talking about it — responsibility, that is. They made it sound as if it were something she didn't know anything about.

"If you ask me, Annie isn't old enough for a job," her father half suggested.

But he didn't interfere. He didn't believe in interfering, Annie thought, a little resentfully, as she walked down to the corner to wait for the bus. Once he had let her climb all the way to the top of the roof without interfering. "If she falls, she falls," he had said, and had gone into the house and closed the door.

She had come down then, slowly and extra carefully. But he could have waited and watched to be sure she was all right. He could have, she thought now. And she dragged the overnight bag up the steps of the bus after her.

5 The Sigbys

THE SIGBY HOUSE had a white picket fence all around it. The porch was swept clean; there was a plastic swan standing on the front lawn, white painted rocks bordering the flower beds around the house, and not a weed anywhere at all. Annie rang the bell.

Its peal sounded sharply through the house. It probably could be heard in the attic, thought Annie, and wondered, with a little stir of excitement, if the Sigbys had an attic. She remembered she had always wanted to live in a house with an attic. Her house was flat-roofed.

She heard footsteps hastening down some stairs. The curtain on the window at the side of the door moved; there was a rustle, a click, and the door opened. Mrs. Sigby peered at her through the screen door.

She wore an apron with flowers on it — the kind Migs' mother always wore, and neat black shoes that tied. There was a brooch pinned to the front of her housedress, and pleased recognition on her face. She smiled and nodded and smiled and nodded, holding the screen door open just wide enough for Annie to come through. The smell of furniture polish wafted out.

Annie took a deep breath, liking it. "I'm here," she said.

"Annie's here, Mr. Sigby!" Mrs. Sigby called over her shoulder. "Annie's here!"

She was small and thin; her voice was thin too, and a little quavery as if with excitement.

She called her husband *Mr. Sigby*, the way Regina sometimes called her mother *Professor* instead of mother. Annie smiled. Her doing that made Mrs. Sigby seem even more like a little girl.

Mr. Sigby came out of a little room off the hallway. It was a narrow hallway, with a very narrow flight of stairs going straight up, guarded by a spindly railing. The first post had a round wooden knob on it, big as a head, and shiny. In Annie's house it would have been the place on which to leave a hat — she thought of her mother, or drape a sweater — her father. In the half light of the hallway, it gleamed baldly; it was a beacon of order at the Sigbys'.

It caught the shine of Mr. Sigby's silver-framed glasses. Behind him, Annie glimpsed a television set, a heavy couch with a fringe cover, and a small oval tippy-looking glass-topped coffee table.

Mr. Sigby had been in there reading — there was a book in his hands, and his finger still marked his place. But he didn't look rumpled as Annie's father did when he was slumped over a book. Mr. Sigby's hair was white and smooth, his sweater neatly buttoned and he even wore a tie. He wore a tie under the collar of his blue shirt just as if he were expecting company!

He stood there smiling and nodding at Annie, too. Mr. Sigby was not at all like Mrs. Sigby, Annie couldn't help but notice. She was short and he was tall. Her thinness gave her a frail look; his leanness made him seem strong. Mrs. Sigby's face was pinkish only at her chin; but Mr. Sigby's was ruddy all over. Even his neck had thick brown folds.

"He's been gardening!" Mrs. Sigby said, with a soft tch, tch of her tongue and her lips. "He's been out since early morning, thinning the radishes, working in the sun."

"It's good for a man to work with his hands," Mr. Sigby said in the softest voice Annie had ever heard. She looked at him in amazement.

"Come in, Annie," he said. "Come in."

Annie put her bag down on the hall rug, and Mrs. Sigby immediately lifted it and shifted it to the bare floor.

They are glad to see me, thought Annie. And suddenly she was more than glad to see them.

Mrs. Sigby bustled around her. She opened the closet door and brought out a hanger. There was a faint smell of moth crystals from inside the hall closet.

Annie sniffed at it pleasurefully.

"You didn't forget to wipe your feet, did you?" Mrs. Sigby said.

Quickly Annie backed out, wiped her feet on the mat, and came in again.

Mr. Sigby nodded approvingly and went back into the small room.

"Hang up your coat," Mrs. Sigby advised. "Use the wooden hanger, the wire ones I save for ironing."

Annie took off her jacket and hung it up.

"I always hang up my coat as soon as I come into the house," Mrs. Sigby said brightly. "That way it hangs out any wrinkles."

"It's a good idea," Annie said earnestly.

"The living room is there," Mrs. Sigby said, pointing to a closed door that slid open. Annie nodded. Mrs. Sigby had told Annie that when she had brought the ad. Mrs. Sigby had been in the living room dusting when Annie had come in through the gate, and she had come out onto the porch to talk to Annie, closing the door carefully behind her. Mrs. Sigby didn't like doors hanging open. She had told Annie that too. She always kept the living room door shut, unless she knew they were expecting company. She and Mr. Sigby usually sat in the little room Mr. Sigby was in. They called it the den.

"Mr. Sigby reads a lot," she said now to Annie.

"My father does too!" Annie said quickly.

"The Bible," Mrs. Sigby said gently. "Mr. Sigby reads a piece out of the Bible every day. He's gotten into the habit of reading out loud." She shut the closet door tight. "He could probably read to you from that Bible with his eyes closed, he's read it so often. The Old Testament," she said proudly. "He's a great one for telling stories out of the Old Testament. Mr. Sigby always says if you want the truth, you can read it in the Bible." Her face was solemn.

Annie listened solemnly too. It was an awesome idea. She had never thought about it that way before. As a matter of fact, she had to admit to herself, she had never thought about the Bible at all — except as a place to press four-leaf clovers.

"He's right too!" said Mrs. Sigby with a firm nod. "You can't believe a word of what you read in the daily newspapers! — that's what my daddy always said."

"That's what my father says too," Annie told her eagerly, though she was aware it wasn't exactly what he had said. Certainly near enough, though.

Mrs. Sigby beamed at her. "The kitchen is at the end of this hall, that door to the back. There's a place out on the back porch to leave your umbrella. Mr. Sigby and I always use the back door. Handier, and it saves cleaning the front hall."

"Oh," said Annie, "I didn't know."

"The garbage man picks up the cans in the back alley, and we hardly ever have things delivered. Mr. Sigby does all the shopping himself." Her voice was full of pride. "He doesn't drive anymore," she explained, "but we have our own grocery cart. He just pushes it up to the nearest supermarket and fills it and pushes it back. It folds up," she added. "Sometimes, he just gets on the bus with it and goes way across town to shop. My, he's a real bargain hunter. Mr. Sigby's been shopping in every supermarket on the bus line! Specials," she said approvingly. "He can tell you to the half cent which stores give the best bargains in specials. He's a very *careful* buyer, you can believe me!"

Annie believed her; it wasn't difficult. She liked Mrs. Sigby. She liked her gentle ways, her neatness, the quick birdlike way she walked, and the emphatic way she talked. It suddenly occurred to Annie that she'd have to keep her dresser drawer extra neat here. She didn't have to see Mrs. Sigby's drawers to know that they were always in perfect order!

"Mr. Sigby and I like things to be orderly."

"Oh I do too!" said Annie.

"We've always believed in promptness," she said. "Mr. Sigby doesn't like lallygagging over the dinner table. He won't stand for anyone being late to the table, or wasting good food once you sit down to eat. Mr. Sigby doesn't hold with people being late for anything. 'Bad as dirt!' he says."

"I'll remember," Annie said.

"Like Mr. Sigby says, there's a right way and a wrong way to do things. You might as well learn to do it the right way, right at the start."

That seemed to make good sense, and Annie nodded. Mrs. Sigby patted Annie's shoulder approvingly. She peered at Annie's face.

"I don't believe in girls making their lips red. It's not natural."

"I never use it!" Annie said hastily, and she wouldn't, she promised herself.

"Girls should be girls, is what Mr. Sigby always says," Mrs. Sigby confided. "And boys should be boys. He can't abide boys with long hair — or girls wearing pants."

Annie looked down at the overnight bag she had brought. It was lucky she had forgotten to pack her jeans.

"Bring up your things," said Mrs. Sigby, leading the way. "I just wanted to be sure you know what kind of people you've come to live with."

Annie followed her up the steep stairway. She tried very hard not to bang her bag against the slim banisters, and instead kept knocking it against her own legs. She stumbled. Mrs. Sigby looked around.

"You've got to be careful of that seventh step — it creaks. I broke my leg on it once, when we first moved here." She looked at it with a kind of satisfaction. Mr. Sigby says he's going to let it creak till doomsday — " she giggled like a little girl. "So it'll be a reminder to me to be extra careful, you know." She stopped at the top of the stairs. "He's a very cautious man, Mr. Sigby is. I always say — he reminds me of my daddy."

The hallway turned in an L. There was another post with a round knob at the head of the stairs. A newel post, Mrs. Sigby called it.

"My daughter Dorothy knocked the top off it once," she said. "It bounced right down to the bottom. It scared her. She thought it was the walls of Jericho falling down!

"It's in the Bible," she said over her shoulder. "The way the horn blew and the people shouted and the walls came tumbling down. It was Dorothy's favorite story. You might say she grew up on it. Mr. Sigby used to tell it to her to put her to sleep."

She stopped to explain, "Dorothy is our daughter. Got two little ones of her own now. Maybe I told you."

"You told me," Annie said politely.

"Well, this is the upstairs."

Annie looked into each of the three bedrooms. The doors were open, not hanging halfway, but propped all the way back.

"Mr. Sigby made the doorstops," Mrs. Sigby said. "He likes to make things. 'A man should work with his hands,' he says. Keeps his tools in the garage. That's what we use the garage for now. The tools. He used to make all sorts of things. The sandbox in the back-yard he made for Dorothy when she was little. We still keep sand in it, like we always did."

The doorstops were smoothly polished wedges.

"We don't like banging doors," Mrs. Sigby said positively. "This room is yours. It used to be Dorothy's."

They were all exactly alike, Annie noticed. Each of the three bedrooms held a double bed, a comforter, a chest of drawers, and white starched curtains. The bedspread in Dorothy's room was pink. "It was always my favorite color," Mrs. Sigby said. "Pink." The wallpaper had been up a long time, thought Annie. It was sort of pink, too.

Annie thought of her own room at home, with the deep double chest, the telephone on its own bedside table, the wild yellow pillows on her bed, and the wallpapered ceiling. She had her own desk and her own shelf of books.

"It's nice," she said, and really meant it. "It's neat
- and well, nice."

"Dorothy always liked it," said Mrs. Sigby. "That's
how I knew you'd like it. You'll be just like one of the
family."

Suddenly there was a lump in Annie's throat. "That's
just what I wanted," she said.

"You just do what you're told and you won't get into
any trouble."

"I know," said Annie. "I'm pleased! I mean I like to
know what's what."

"That's what my daddy always told me," said little
Mrs. Sigby. "Just do what you're told and you'll get
along all right."

Annie smiled. "That'll be easy," she said happily.

6 The Schedule

"THEY DON'T SMOKE," Annie said importantly to her mother. "They don't drink — " she glanced sideways at the glass on the table next to her father's chair — "not even coffee!"

Her father put his book face down over his knee and used the eraser end of his pencil to rub at the middle of the bald spot on his head. He regarded her curiously.

"How did you ever happen to find a family like that!" her mother asked.

Annie couldn't help smiling to herself. "I guess I was just lucky," she said earnestly, and tried not to mind her mother's sudden laughter.

Mrs. Sigby never laughed like that. Annie didn't say so, of course, but anybody could see that Mrs. Sigby thought it unladylike to laugh out so loud. Mrs. Sigby barely talked in a whisper most of the time. Annie winced a little at the loud tone of her mother's voice.

"We have a schedule," she told them, not trying to hide the pride in her voice. "We have to get up at exactly seven-thirty. Breakfast is at eight-thirty; lunch at a quarter-past twelve and dinner six sharp."

"You mean everybody *has* to eat breakfast at exactly

eight-thirty?" Howard sounded as if it were a silly idea.

"Nobody *ever* comes downstairs in their bathrobes," Annie said pointedly.

"Why not?" Howard who had come down in his pajama bottoms only, without any bathrobe, stared hard at her.

"They're not allowed," Annie said, rather pleased with the sound of it. "I'm not allowed to do *anything* anybody else in the family isn't supposed to do."

"Very liberal idea," said Mr. Lee dryly.

Annie looked at him quickly. Sometimes it was hard to tell whether her father was agreeing or disagreeing. She didn't have that trouble with Mr. Sigby. Everyone knew when he was in disagreement. His voice didn't slide down at the ends of his sentences. His words didn't get chewed up and mumbled away during a discourse. He didn't lecture. When Mr. Sigby spoke up, it was firm and clear. Everyone listened when Mr. Sigby said anything.

"What do they think about the President's Foreign Policy program?" Howard wanted to know.

"How would I know?" said Annie.

"Well, don't they talk?"

"Sure they talk. Mrs. Sigby talks all the time." Then she felt a little disloyal for saying that.

"I'm sure it must be a very nice family," Mrs. Lee said as if she didn't think so at all.

"You don't have to like them," Annie reminded. "*I* like them."

"That's what's most important, I guess," her mother said.

"You haven't looked at my gerbils," Howard reminded her. "A pair. Male and female. They had babies the day after I put them in the cage. I named them Geoffrey, Geribaldi, Gertrude — "

"And Gunther!" Mrs. Lee supplied enthusiastically.

"Six? What are you going to do with six?" Annie said.

"There were eight," Howard said. "Two of them died. Do you want to see them?"

"Not if they're dead!" said Annie.

Her mother laughed.

Annie frowned. "I have to go over and see Migs," she said, and she went out the front door and across the street.

Migs' mother opened the door for her. "Migs is upstairs in her room," she said.

"Come on up!" shouted Migs.

"Excuse me," Annie said politely as she went around Migs' mother and up the stairs.

"I'm not going to camp after all," Migs said happily.

"I thought you said your mother said you had to go."

"She changed her mind. She heard they were having boys the same time as girls. She didn't see any sense to that. It's not a Catholic camp."

"I see," said Annie, but she was not sure she did at all.

"Are you going back to your job?"

"I like it!"

"What do you have to do?"

"Just help. Just like the ad said. Mrs. Sigby tells me what to do every day and I do it. It's easy."

"What's it like?"

"Well, it's not like home I can tell you that!"

Carefully she took off her shoes and sat on Migs' bed.

"You don't ever have to worry about forgetting! Mrs. Sigby keeps reminding you all the time."

"That sounds like my mother!" said Migs.

"Mrs. Sigby believes in strict rules!"

"Familiar!" said Migs.

"You can't do this and you can't do that!" said Annie happily.

Migs groaned. "You poor thing!"

Annie giggled. "I'm not even allowed to read in bed!"

"*My* mother isn't letting me take out any more library books if I get one more overdue!"

"Mr. Sigby never takes books from the library," Annie said quickly. "He's always reading to us from the Bible!"

Migs stared at her respectfully.

"He's on the part about Isaac and Rebekah and how they had twins Esau and Jacob, only Esau was born first. And Esau was big and Jacob was little. But Jacob was smarter than Esau and he bought Esau's birthright from him for a bowl of pottage."

"You mean you have to sit there and just listen!"

"In the den!" Annie said. "We're not allowed to sit in the living room unless there is company."

"My mother doesn't believe I should have any company at all!" Migs said darkly. "Tom Jacobsen came over yesterday and she didn't even let me invite him in! Suppose someone came all the way on the bus just to see you — wouldn't you think you could ask him in!"

"I guess I wouldn't be allowed," Annie said promptly.

Migs made a face. "Last night he called at exactly six o'clock. My mother wouldn't even call me to the telephone!"

"Why not?"

"She won't let us go to the telephone when we're eating dinner."

"Mrs. Sigby won't let me use the telephone at all unless it's an emergency," Annie said quickly.

"Well, if Tom Jacobsen called you I guess you'd consider it important enough to call it an emergency," Migs said.

"Dorothy wasn't allowed to use the telephone either!"

"Dorothy who?"

"That's Mr. and Mrs. Sigby's daughter. She's married now. I sleep in the room that was hers. Pink."

"Oh, I like pink!"

"You wouldn't like this pink," said Annie. "To tell you the truth, I can't understand why I like it."

"Maybe it's because you didn't have to choose it yourself," said Migs.

Annie lay back and grinned at the ceiling. "I guess that's it," she said happily. "Did I tell you we have to eat cereal every morning?"

"Hot?"

Annie nodded.

"So do we," Migs said. "My mother won't let me leave the table until I've finished every lump!"

Annie closed Migs' bedroom door behind her and went down the stairs. There was a rag rug on the landing. Migs' mother had made it out of old stockings. Annie stood there a moment and gazed at it. The red must be Migs' old knee-lengths, she decided, and the brown would be Robert's. She felt a sharp sting on her cheek, and bent to pick up a rubber band that had been shot at her from behind the upstairs railing.

Another rubber band landed at her feet. She looked quickly over her shoulder, and sniffed. Chest rub.

"You stop that, Robert!" she shouted.

Migs' mother came around from the kitchen and started up the stairs. She was carrying a pile of folded sheets and towels. She looked at Annie sharply.

"I'm just going," Annie said, and hurried on down the stairs and out.

The upstairs window opened. "Hey, Annie!" Robert's voice flung out at her.

She crossed the street, not even bothering to turn around.

"You mean you're going to stay there all summer!" Migs had said.

"Maybe even longer," Annie had answered recklessly.

Suddenly she couldn't help smiling.

7 —And Gunther

"At the Sigbys' we always say Grace first," said Annie, when they sat down for dinner.

"Pass the potatoes," Howard said.

"Why don't you say it for us," Mrs. Lee suggested.

Annie bent her head until she felt her chin brush against her collar. She thought for a moment and said in a respectful and hushed tone: "O Lord, we thank you for this food you have provided for us and ask your forgiveness for all the times we have forgotten to mention it."

"Oh Lord!" said Howard.

Annie frowned at him. "Everybody is supposed to say Amen."

"Pass the potatoes," her father said.

Her mother said judiciously — "It certainly doesn't hurt anyone to stop and think about his blessings now and then."

"There are times when I'm tempted to stop and question some of mine," her father said.

Annie looked at her parents impatiently. They had forgotten all about saying Amen. Her father was mashing butter into his mashed potatoes. He leaned on the table; his shirt collar was unbuttoned, and his sleeves were rolled up.

"Mr. and Mrs. Sigby *dress* for dinner!"

Her father peered around. "It doesn't appear to me that anyone of us is sitting here naked," he said mildly.

Her mother laughed.

Her mother always laughed at anything her father said, Annie thought. It didn't seem to Annie that her father was that funny.

"Good pot roast," observed Mr. Lee. "Spicy! Excellent!"

"That's what it's called," Annie's mother sounded pleased. "Spicy pot roast. It's a new recipe."

"Mrs. Sigby never uses spices. Just salt and pepper," Annie said.

Howard stood up. His father looked at him inquiringly. "The gerbils." he said. "I just remembered I forgot to feed the gerbils." He picked up his glass of milk and took a long gulp. "They like lettuce," he said importantly, "and dog food." He pinched off a bit of meat with his fingers. "They're crazy about bird seeds too."

"They sound a little crazy, all right, to me," Annie said.

"If you want to pick one up, the best way to get a hold is by its tail," Howard advised.

"No thank you!" Annie called after him hastily.

"They're not at all timid," Mr. Lee said. "The dickens to catch, but once you've got hold of one, it enjoys being petted."

"Kids are sometimes like that too." Mrs. Lee was smiling.

An odd sound came from upstairs. Mr. Lee listened toward the ceiling, scratching his nose.

Howard came running down. "They're gone!" he shouted.

"What do you mean 'gone'?" Mrs. Lee was shouting too.

Mr. Lee slid out of his chair without moving it and started upstairs.

"The baby gerbils! Someone must have gone in to look at them and let the babies out!" Howard looked accusingly at Annie.

"I didn't touch them!" Annie said. "I don't like gerbils anyway. I wouldn't touch them even if I wanted to!"

"Someone touched them!"

Their father appeared at the top of the stairs. He held the cage in his hands. It was a wooden box covered in the front with a wire mesh. It must have been an old bookcase. In it were only two gerbils. They were tiny furry animals.

"The mother," he said with a strange grimace. "She ate them."

There was a shocked silence. Then Mrs. Lee said incredulously, "She *ate* them?"

"I think I've heard of it," said Mr. Lee. His face was twisted as if he were trying to recall a page out of a book. "The female gerbil sometimes eats her babies —

particularly if she's startled or scared. Loud noises will do it, I suppose. Let's face it — when you're a baby gerbil, your greatest enemy is your mother."

"That's not funny," said Mrs. Lee.

"I read that they don't like strangers either," Mr. Lee said. "You stick a strange gerbil child in with another family, and the whole family have been known to chase it until it's dead."

Annie shuddered.

"I wonder why they keep on having babies," said Howard.

"Nature," said his father. "Nature does a lot of curious things."

"Well, I'm glad I'm not a gerbil," Annie said.

"Some human mothers aren't much different," her father said with a grimace. "They don't want their children to grow up. They keep them dependent. You could say — they *swallow* their offspring."

"But that's not really eating them!"

"In a manner of speaking, it is. They just gobble them up, euphemistically speaking."

"How do you spell that?" Howard inquired.

"G-o-b-b-l-e," Annie said.

"I mean euphe — whatever it was." Howard pulled the dictionary out from under the coffee table.

"Euphemistically," his mother said. "A euphemism is saying something not very good in a way that makes it sound better."

Howard rapidly turned the pages — " '*Euphemism*

— ' " he read. "Hey! That's right. That's exactly what it does mean."

"I don't think gobbling sounds any better than eating and swallowing," said Annie.

"Anyway, now we know what to expect of gerbils!" her mother said.

"I have to be back before four," Annie said loudly.

Howard went back upstairs and came down again. He carried an encyclopedia with him. "They should be having babies pretty soon again," he said hopefully. "Some gerbils reproduce every six weeks."

"Lordy!" said her mother. "I can see how she might consider them expendable!"

Howard picked up his dictionary again and began to turn the pages.

"E-x-p — " said his mother.

Annie glanced at her watch.

"It's two o'clock," Howard said helpfully.

"You don't have to be back before four," her father said, as if he were just repeating something he had heard and it didn't matter very much.

Annie frowned carefully at her wristwatch. "I mustn't be late," she said.

"You certainly mustn't," her mother said rather peculiarly.

Annie looked at her suspiciously.

Mrs. Lee glanced at her own watch. "That's funny, mine says six o'clock."

Annie jumped up. "Six o'clock!"

"I guess I forgot to wind it," Mrs. Lee said, and Howard laughed.

Annie didn't sit down. "I'll just *die* if I'm late."

An odd sound came from Mr. Lee's throat. "Pardon me," he said then quickly, and opened his book.

"Annie in Sigby land," Howard said. "Ohdearohdearohdear!" he squeaked. "I'm going to be late."

Nobody reproved him. Neither her mother nor her father.

Annie turned her back on all three of them.

When she got off the bus, she found herself hurrying down the street toward the white picket gate. She latched it carefully behind her and went around to the back door.

"Here's Annie," Mr. Sigby said from the den.

"You didn't forget to wipe your feet, did you?" Mrs. Sigby called out.

Annie had to smile. "I remembered!" she sang out dutifully. She sniffed the faint smell of polished furniture coming from the living room, and the odor of moth crystals from the hall closet.

"Hang up your coat," Mrs. Sigby advised. "Use the wooden hanger, the wire ones I save for ironing."

"I have already," Annie said, enjoying the familiar sound of the words.

"I always hang up my coat as soon as I come into the house. That way it hangs out any wrinkles."

"I know," Annie said.

She moved to the door of the den and looked in,

smiling at them. Mrs. Sigby was sitting in the big chair with her ankles crossed and her hands folded. Mr. Sigby held his Bible open on his lap.

"You're just in time," he said as if he were glad to see her.

"Sit down, Annie," Mrs. Sigby said.

Annie sat down.

"We always read every Sunday evening from the Bible," Mrs. Sigby said.

Annie nodded.

"If you want the truth, you can read it in the Bible, that's what I always say," said Mr. Sigby.

"We've been waiting for you," Mrs. Sigby said, and settled her shoulders back into the cushion of the chair.

"I'm glad you did!" For some reason Annie felt a lump in her throat.

Mr. Sigby put on his glasses and began in his reading voice —

"When Isaac was old and his eyes were dim so that he could not see, he called Esau his older son and said to him —"

Mrs. Sigby began to rock in her chair. It made a rhythmic squeak, punctuation marks to Mr. Sigby's deep soft voice *". . . that I may bless you before I die."*

Annie took a slow deep breath. She guessed she had heard the story before, but she had never really listened to it. Esau was his father's favorite, and Jacob was his mother's favorite. And when Isaac sent Esau out to hunt some food to give him strength to give the blessing, Rebekah called Jacob. She sent Jacob to his father,

Isaac — dressed in Esau's clothes . . . Annie listened as Mr. Sigby read on in his slow steady voice . . . *"so he blessed him."*

Jacob instead of Esau, thought Annie. She guessed Esau had forgotten that he had sold his birthright to Jacob. But Jacob hadn't forgotten.

Unaccountably, Annie felt a yawn coming on. She twisted her mouth around trying to hold it in, and the effort tickled her nostrils. She rubbed hard at her nose with her handkerchief.

"You've not gone and caught cold, have you?" Mrs. Sigby was looking at her worriedly.

"I'm sure I haven't!"

"I used to get terrible colds when I was your age," Mrs. Sigby said.

"I never catch colds," Annie said reassuringly.

"You'd better take two aspirins before you go to bed," Mrs. Sigby said. "You can take a half a lemon and squeeze it into a glass and add some water and honey and that will make you feel better, too."

"I feel fine!"

"Now don't go walking around in your bedroom in bare feet," Mrs. Sigby called after her when she went up to bed. "It could turn into pneumonia in no time."

Annie grinned as she ran up the stairs. It was good to be *home*.

8   The Strange Person

Mrs. Sigby kept her doors locked the next day. All of them. She went around the house making sure all the windows were closed tightly too. "You can't be too careful," she warned Annie. "Mr. Sigby said he saw a *person* lurking around here last night."

"A person?" Annie looked out the window. "What kind of a person?"

"The worst kind!" Mr. Sigby said, coming into the kitchen. "I don't like tramps. Never did and never will! The Lord gave us two strong arms to work with and anyone who doesn't choose to work can starve, so far as He and I are concerned."

Annie looked at him in surprise. Her father sometimes referred to God and himself, together, but only in fun. She looked carefully at Mr. Sigby. His mouth was pressed tight and his eyes gleamed hard and steadily. Mr. Sigby meant exactly what he said.

Mrs. Sigby peered out the kitchen window worriedly. "It's terrible when good people can't go out of their own houses safely."

"We didn't have television and bombs and things like

that when I was a boy," Mr. Sigby said. "We didn't go sticking our nose in other people's business either. Kids didn't get away with trying to tell the President how to run the country. And if a stranger came sneaking up to the yard late at night you could call the police and they would throw him in jail."

"Did you call the police?" asked Mrs. Sigby.

"Reported it straight off," said Mr. Sigby. "They wrote it down. Leastways, they said they were writing it down. They said there weren't enough policemen on the whole force to investigate every complaint. That's all they said."

Mrs. Sigby turned away from the window. "You mean we got to wait till someone hits us over the head or breaks in and robs us, before the police will do anything about it!"

"But the police can't arrest someone who hasn't done anything!" Annie said, feeling puzzled.

"Why not!" Mrs. Sigby demanded in her thin voice. "If we know they might! Why not?"

"But that's just it — how would you *know*?"

Mr. Sigby was looking at her disapprovingly. He didn't like questions like that.

"You shouldn't be talking about things you're too young to understand," Mrs. Sigby said.

But Annie went on thinking about it. "I suppose there's some kind of law about trespassing. Was the person trespassing? I mean, did he come into the yard or anything!"

"He didn't so much as set foot on the sidewalk in

front of the house," Mr. Sigby said with satisfaction. "I saw to that!"

Mrs. Sigby regarded him proudly. "Now don't you worry, Annie." She seemed to be shedding her worry like an uncomfortable sweater. "So long as Mr. Sigby's taken care of it, neither of us has to worry."

"I'm not worrying," said Annie. "I was just thinking about it."

"Well, there are some things young girls shouldn't even think about!" Mrs. Sigby said. She bustled around taking things out of cupboards and opening and closing drawers. "We're going to can today. We always start our canning this time of year."

"Did you tell Annie about the telephone call?" Mr. Sigby said.

"What telephone call?" Annie turned around.

"She said to tell you it was Migs."

"She lives across the street from me," Annie said.

"I told her of course that you couldn't come to the phone. It was almost ten o'clock."

"One minute to," said Mr. Sigby.

"We always turn off the lights at ten o'clock," said Mrs. Sigby.

"She's my very best friend!"

"Well, she was very nice and polite, I'll say that for her."

"Her mother is very strict! She can't go anywhere without asking her mother first."

"I don't believe in young girls going out after dark alone," said Mrs. Sigby. "I never did."

"Migs can't even go anywhere in the afternoon without telling her mother first!"

Mrs. Sigby gave her an approving nod. "She sounds like a nice friend."

"As soon as I'm through with my work, I'll call her." Annie hoped Mrs. Sigby had noticed her admirable attention to duty.

"Won't do you much good," Mrs. Sigby said. "She's not going to be home. That's what she wanted to tell you."

Annie hummed a little as she carefully carried the blue breakfast dishes to the sink. She wiped each cup with special attention, and placed each spoon in its proper row in the drawer.

"I'm glad to see you're feeling much better today," Mrs. Sigby observed.

"I feel just fine!" Annie said happily.

Mrs. Sigby nodded. "I thought you would. Nothing like a good night's sleep and a little honey and aspirin to keep off a cold. Dorothy never had a cold in her life!"

Annie smiled to herself. "What do I do next?" She waited obediently at the sink, although she knew that the table was to be wiped and the dish towels would have to be rinsed out and hung to dry.

"The table," directed Mrs. Sigby, importantly. "The sponge is under the sink. Rinse it out well! I always wipe the table with a little polish every day."

"I know," said Annie, and proceeded to do it, just as she had done every morning since she had come to the

Sigbys'. She wiped the table the way Mrs. Sigby told her, working from the center to the edges, and down the legs too.

"Rinse the dish towels out in the sink," said Mrs. Sigby, "and hang them on the line out on the porch."

Mrs. Sigby never expected her to remember anything, thought Annie happily. It seemed easy and pleasant to move mechanically, doing only what she was told to do.

She gave the wet dish towels an efficient flap, and stretched them onto the line. She could see all of the neat backyard — Dorothy's sandbox, and Mr. Sigby's vegetable garden and the back alley. The sun was shining brightly; there was no one at all around.

"The birds are singing," she reported, as she came in and closed the door behind her.

Mrs. Sigby was getting out the canning kettle and nodded her usual nod of approval, as if the birds too had been following her direction.

"I don't believe in letting anything go to waste," Mrs. Sigby said. "Why I got plum jam down in the basement that I put up three years ago. Plenty of starving people would be tickled to death to have what I have down in the basement I can tell you that."

"Peas," Mr. Sigby reported, coming in from the outside. He took off his shoes and left them on the porch. "Beans. The cucumbers aren't ripe yet, and corn will be late."

"I have plenty of jamming to do." Mrs. Sigby hurried from the table to the sink. "We always make plum jam and jelly too," she told Annie. "I put up applesauce and apple butter every year. We do tomatoes every other year."

"Tomatoes don't look so good to me this year," Mr. Sigby said.

"We always do tomatoes every other year," she scolded.

He opened the basement door. "I'd better bring up the jars."

Mrs. Sigby nodded, glancing once again toward the window. "I don't believe in strays," she said positively. "Not cats, nor dogs, nor people. There should be a special place for them is what I say."

"There's the pound for cats and dogs," Annie said.

"And the jail for people," Mr. Sigby reminded her.

Annie said doubtfully — "I don't think you can put people in jail just for walking around."

"Well, they should!" said Mrs. Sigby with a sniff. "Just like cats and dogs. They should!"

Over her head, Mrs. Sigby smiled at Annie. She smiled back. Dear little Mrs. Sigby — she could hardly imagine anyone being bad and human at the same time!

Annie helped all morning. She washed out jars that already looked clean. Mrs. Sigby inspected approvingly, while Annie scrubbed hard at the inside of each one.

Mr. Sigby looked in with his Bible under his arm. "Call me if you see any strangers around," he advised. "I'll deal with them!"

Mrs. Sigby looked after him fondly. "I don't know what I'd do without Mr. Sigby." She shook her head at her own helplessness.

She's sweet, thought Annie. She's really motherly! And for some reason the thought of her own mother — big and handsome with a loud voice and firm opinions — rose before her. She put her whole attention on cleaning the jars.

"God gave men the brains and women the beauty — that's what my daddy always said," said Mrs. Sigby. "And I guess it's right."

Annie nodded, a little self-consciously. She had never thought of herself as even *pretty*.

She helped Mrs. Sigby ladle the hot fruit into the jars, and later, carried the jars down to the basement. It was a clean basement, the cleanest she had ever seen. Everything stored down there was wrapped in paper, or put in boxes, or covered with plastic sheets. A clean old tablecloth hung over the washing machine.

There were even curtains on the windows, though the floor was bare cement and the furnace stood right out in the middle. It had round pipes coming out of the top like a sprouting onion. Mrs. Sigby's laundry tubs and washing machine took up one end of the basement, and the fruit shelves the other. In one corner there was a stack of newspapers reaching almost as high as the windowsill, and an old kitchen chair.

"I have to climb on the chair to dust those pipes up there," explained Mrs. Sigby.

"You dust the furnace!"

"It gets dirty." Mrs. Sigby picked up the chair and set it down next to the fruit shelves.

Annie ran to help her. "It's a lovely basement!" she said sincerely.

"We never had mice," Mrs. Sigby said proudly. "Mr. Sigby thinks there is no excuse for mice."

Annie chuckled, but Mrs. Sigby was too busy counting the jars to see how funny that had sounded.

Mrs. Sigby kept lists. There was one inside the kitchen, next to the sink. There was one in the hall closet. There was one tacked up on the back porch. And there was one here in the basement too. Mrs. Sigby was adding items to it now.

"When you write down something you don't have to worry about remembering it," Mrs. Sigby said.

"That's so!" Annie said.

"Dorothy is coming next week," Mr. Sigby said after dinner.

"She can use the other bedroom. You can put a cot in it for Hubert," Mrs. Sigby told him.

"Hubert and Sylvia. Hubert's the boy and Sylvia's the girl," said Mr. Sigby. "Look like Dorothy's husband, Henry."

"Dorothy always took after Mr. Sigby," said Mrs. Sigby with real pride. "People always said she was her father to a T."

"She was a good girl," Mr. Sigby said gravely. "Always did what she was told."

Mrs. Sigby nodded too.

That was high praise, thought Annie. It was about the highest praise Mr. and Mrs. Sigby could give.

Conscientiously, Annie began to make a list of her own that night. With good intention, she put down all the rules Mrs. Sigby had given her.

She started with — Use the back door, not the front. Carefully she wrote down — Wipe your feet before you come in. Hang up your coat so that wrinkles will hang out. Use wooden hanger. The blue dishes for breakfast. The white dishes for dinner. Don't talk at the dinner table. Get up at seven-thirty. Don't be late!!! Be careful of the seventh step. No lights on after ten o'clock, *positively!* — and underlined that three times.

The list was reaching to the end of the page. She turned the paper over. She added Mrs. Sigby's admonitions for setting the table, clearing it, and the order of doing the dishes. (Wash glasses first!) Mrs. Sigby didn't believe in dishwashers. She continued on with the precise way dishes must be stacked in the cupboards (every cup on its own saucer) and on through the usual duties of the day. She came to the bottom of the page and read it all through with satisfaction. Then she set the paper up against the mirror on her bureau where she could see it from any place in the room. She walked back and forth in front of it, feeling pleased with it, and with herself.

She got into bed, turned off her light before Mrs. Sigby tapped on her door in reminder, and lay there for a moment in a blissful blankness. She didn't have to think about anything, she reminded herself, it was all there on the list!

She got up hurriedly then and added one more item — Beware of strangers!

9 A Kiss, a Wrangle

ROBERT WAS SITTING on his porch steps when she got off the bus. He galloped over.

"Your mother said she thought you were coming home soon, all right!" He stared at her happily.

"I *always* come home for my day off on the three-fifteen." It was almost exactly the way Mrs. Sigby said, "We always use the blue dishes for breakfast."

"Well, she must have forgot," said Robert. "She said to tell you they'd be home pretty soon. They went downtown."

"All of them?"

"Your brother is at the library." Robert scratched his head. "Or maybe it was your father who was at the library."

Annie smiled, and he smiled too.

She sat down on the step and he stood looking down at her a little while. It made her uneasy, his standing over her. She twitched and moved over. "You might as well sit down," she said.

He sat down. Close to her. She moved a little, turning her head away from the smell of chest rub. She guessed Robert was the one who was always catching cold. She heard him breathing through his mouth next to her neck and she turned her head. His face was next to hers. Then he kissed her. Well, she guessed it was a kiss — he plopped his lips on her cheek — and so it must have been that.

"What did you do that for?" she said.

He grinned. "It's all right, nobody's home."

She didn't say anything. She didn't have to say anything, for the window in the upstairs bedroom across the street opened and Migs' mother hollered out —

"Rob — BERT!"

He almost fell off the porch. He moved quickly away from Annie. "I'm here!" he yelled back.

"I know where you are!" she said ominously. "Come right home!"

He went. He got up off her porch steps and went. He didn't even look back.

Annie shrugged and went into the house. Everything was the same. The coat closet hung open. There was a pile of books on the living room floor, her father's slippers lay upside down on the sofa cushion, her mother's gloves had been left on the table, and an ashtray on the floor. She went upstairs into her bedroom and shut the door behind her.

"How's it feel coming home like a visitor?" Migs asked her the next day. They were sitting on Migs' porch. Annie hadn't seen Robert. She hadn't seen him all day.

"That's right," Annie said.

Migs looked at her blankly.

"That's what I feel like, a visitor. It's hard to believe I ever lived here." She squinted over at her own house across the street. "I bet I could come walking into my house stark naked and hardly anybody would notice."

"If you did my mother probably wouldn't let me go around with you anymore. I have trouble enough with her as it is!" Migs said.

Annie regarded her intently out of the corner of her eyes.

"She hasn't exactly said I shouldn't be going with you. But she's hinted. She says your sister Regina was a real quiet girl — always studying."

"There's nothing quiet about Howard," Annie pointed out. "Your mother likes *him*."

"He's a boy," said Migs. As if that were a perfectly reasonable answer. "She says you're always doing some fool thing. Like the time your mother was airing out all the mattresses in your house and you came along and piled them on top of each other and climbed up and wouldn't come down."

"But I did come down," Annie put in a quick defense. "I fell down!"

"That's what she means," said Migs. "Your mother had to call the fire department. You lost your breath."

"Well, she doesn't have to like me," said Annie.

"Yes she does. Because if she doesn't I can't ask you to my house anymore. I'm not sure she's going to let me ask you to our house anymore as it is! One thing for sure — she's not letting Robert go over to your house soon again!"

Annie looked at her in surprise.

Migs whispered loudly — "She saw you kissing him!"

"I didn't kiss him, he kissed me!"

Migs shrugged. "It's always the girl's fault," she said with a virtuous air. "My mother says so."

Annie stood up. She walked down the steps. She went down the path to the sidewalk, crossed the street, and into her own house.

Resolutely she closed the door behind her.

"Who is that?" her mother called from upstairs.

"It's me," said Annie hoarsely.

"Oh, it's you, Annie." Her mother sounded disappointed, thought Annie.

She marched into the living room. Howard came in through the back door. Her father was sunk into the big chair, reading. He looked a little rumpled, the way he always did. The hair around his bald spot on the top of his head was standing up straight, as it usually was. Her mother came down the stairs.

Annie stared glumly at her plate most of the way through dinner.

"Who'd Mr. Sigby vote for in the last election?" Howard asked.

"How would I know?" she answered.

"Well, is he a Democrat or a Republican?"

"I'll ask him," she said with fine sarcasm. "I'll tell him my little eleven-year-old brother wants to know."

Her father looked at her with a funny expression on his face.

"They don't talk about politics at dinner," she said. "They never discuss things like that when they're eating."

"What do they discuss?" her mother asked curiously.

"Mr. Sigby doesn't allow anyone to talk about anything at all. Dinner is for eating, he says."

Her brother snorted.

"Every summer they put up pickles and peaches and spinach and everything else. They have a basement full of canned goods and preserves."

"Everybody these days freezes things," her mother observed.

"The Sigbys don't," Annie said.

"We don't have a basement," Howard remarked.

"That's what I mean," said Annie significantly.

"What do you mean — 'that's what I mean'?" her mother said.

"I mean — what if there should be a bombing or something like that. What would we do?"

"What do you think we would do?" her father asked. "Now just think about it. What do you think we would do?"

"I don't know," Annie said quickly, almost triumphantly.

Howard looked at his father expectantly. The water in the teakettle began to whistle. Mrs. Lee waited too.

Mr. Lee held up his cup. "Tea?"

Mrs. Lee rose slowly. "I was waiting to hear your answer to Annie."

"I've already answered."

"But you only said —" began Annie in righteous protest.

"— as well as I know how to answer," he added. He smiled wryly. "I know this is hard for you to believe, but I don't know all the answers. There are some things no one — not even I — can answer."

Her mother laughed appreciatively.

"Mr. Sigby does," Annie said quickly. "He knows what's important anyway."

Mr. Lee frowned.

"Nobody has to know the answers to everything anymore," Howard said complacently. "Not with computers around."

"But people still have to do their own thinking," Mr. Lee said. "No computer's been made yet to *think* for anyone. Thinking, and making decisions is still the prerogative of man."

"You don't have to decide about anything when you live at the Sigbys'," Annie said. "You just have to do what you're told."

"Pass the asparagus," her father said.

"It's a very strict family," Annie let the satisfaction show in her voice. "They have a schedule for everything — for getting up, for eating, for going to bed, even for reading . . ."

"Do they have a schedule for going to the bathroom?" Her father's voice was challenging and loud.

It didn't seem funny to Annie, but Howard laughed.

"They're religious!" she threw out at them, as if that

proved something. "I mean — really religious. Mr. Sigby reads out loud from the Bible every Sunday. Nobody says Hell, or Damn, or anything like that."

"Hell," said her father, and began to eat his asparagus.

"They don't believe in allowing kids to go to the movies," she said. "They don't believe in lipstick or going to dances."

"Have some more asparagus," said her mother.

Annie looked around and noted Howard's coat hanging over the back of the chair, her mother's magazines on the floor, and her father's bedroom slippers still on the living room sofa.

"*Their* living room is always nice for company," she couldn't stop herself from saying. "Nobody *ever* comes downstairs without a shirt; *everybody* eats lunch at the same time; all the dishes are washed *immediately* after a meal —"

"Enough!" shouted her father.

Annie snapped her mouth shut. She was frightened but a little pleased too at her father's sudden anger.

"You like that!" His eyes were hard and blue and his chin thrust firm.

Annie swallowed. "That's the way it should be!"

Annie's father made a funny sound in his throat.

Her mother said not very loudly, "Now, Arthur."

The silence ticked around the table.

"Will you please pass the asparagus," Annie said because all of a sudden she didn't know what to say. She nodded at the bowl at her father's elbow.

He went right on eating as if he hadn't heard her.

"I said," she said a little louder, "will you please —"

"Here!" Howard brusquely shoved it over to her.

But the pain in Annie's throat had sharpened and she couldn't eat any more. Her father wouldn't speak to her. He wasn't going to speak to her anymore!

He didn't even raise his head when she came in to say goodbye to them.

"I won't be home next weekend." There seemed to be a strange tightness on the inside of her throat. "Mrs. Sigby said her daughter was coming for a visit and naturally they'll expect me to stay and help them."

"We won't expect you then," her mother said clearly.

Her father didn't say anything at all.

"Gina is coming home next weekend!" Howard yelled after her.

But that thought only made her run faster. She ran as fast as she could, and jumped onto the bus. With Gina there, they wouldn't care if she were not home for the weekend. They wouldn't think about her at all.

10   "Ask, Don't Think!"

It was raining. It was raining the kind of rain it rains sometimes in the middle of summer. It rained like that all morning.

"A regular flood," said Mr. Sigby.

Any rain that kept up for more than a few minutes was a regular flood to Mr. Sigby.

"I think I'll go for a walk," Annie said impulsively.

"In the rain?"

Annie smiled at Mr. Sigby's disbelieving face.

"I like the rain," she said.

"You'll get wet!" Mrs. Sigby said.

"I don't mind," she said gayly, and grabbed her scarf and went out.

She could feel them watching her through the window, and she turned and waved her arm. They didn't wave back.

It was hardly raining at all, she decided.

"It's hardly raining at all," a girl said, coming out of a bakery, looking back at her companion.

Annie didn't know the girl, but the boy was Tom

Jacobsen. She stopped still, unintentionally bumping into the girl.

"Pardon me!" said the girl. "I guess I wasn't looking where I was going!"

"Hi," said Annie to Tom Jacobsen.

"Hi," he said, hardly looking at her. He was pulling a wrapper off a bar of candy.

She watched them walk on down the street. Tom said something and the girl laughed. Then the girl said something and Tom laughed. Back and forth that went all the way up the block.

She walked along looking into store windows, watching them. Every time they stopped, she stopped, and stared at whatever was displayed in the window.

They turned suddenly and started back, and she stood at a shoe repair shop window studying the sign taped to the window inside.

FOR SALE. BABY COBRAS. $2 EACH.

"Cobras!" the girl said stopping right behind Annie. "I wouldn't take one if you gave it to me!"

Annie dug her hands into her pockets.

Tom nudged Annie. "I bet they wouldn't scare you!" he said.

She shrugged. "I was just thinking — it would make a nice birthday gift."

The girl shivered. "I can't think of anyone who'd want a cobra for a birthday gift!"

"If you're the kind who likes alligators, I guess you'd like cobras, wouldn't you?"

"I've never met anyone who likes alligators," Tom said.

"I met a boy yesterday who said he'd sell me some gerbils," the girl said. "They're cute, and they don't smell. Anyway, he said they don't smell."

Annie looked at her quickly. "Maybe that was my brother."

"He said if I wanted them I could have the cage too. It didn't look to me like much of a cage."

Annie said, "That was my brother, all right."

"How do you know?" said Tom.

"I just know."

Tom looked thoughtfully at the shoes in the window. "Personally, I'd just as soon have a cobra."

"So would I!" said Annie promptly.

The girl looked at them both a little suspiciously, and Annie laughed.

She was almost late. She peered in at the Sigbys' kitchen window, stamping her feet on the mat of the back porch.

Mrs. Sigby hurried into the kitchen at the sound.

"Take your shoes off!" she called through the kitchen window.

Annie pulled them off. She took off her wet scarf too and hung it on the porch railing. Then Mrs. Sigby carefully opened the door.

"You'd better sit there out of any draft," Mrs. Sigby fussed. "I'll get you a cup of hot chocolate."

"I'm not cold," Annie protested.

"I always take a cup of hot chocolate when I've been caught in the rain," said Mrs. Sigby.

"It's summer," said Annie. "It's not cold outside at all."

"Summer rains can be worse for you than anything," Mrs. Sigby shook her head emphatically.

Annie sat down and obediently drank the hot chocolate Mrs. Sigby prepared for her. She drank it and thought about Tom Jacobsen.

Mrs. Sigby's daughter arrived late that afternoon. She got out of her car with a basket and an umbrella and two bundled-up children and they all came around to the back door. She was as tall as Mr. Sigby.

"And this is Annie," Mrs. Sigby said, after she had hugged her grandchildren.

"She ought to be a big help to you," Dorothy said grudgingly, as if Annie were not there.

"Hello Hubert, hello Sylvia," Annie said to the two children. They stared at her.

"Now you run along with Annie!" their mother directed, and she and Mrs. Sigby went on upstairs.

Annie took them into the den. "Would you like me to tell you a story?" she asked.

Hubert shook his head.

She sat there looking at them a moment. They stared back at her. They reminded her of Migs' little sisters. Migs' sisters were always out in their backyard playing in the sandbox.

"We'll go outside and play," Annie said brightly.

They didn't protest.

She hustled them into the hallway, and opened the closet door. They stood there while she put them into their sweaters. "You won't need your jackets," she said, and led the way.

She gave them each an empty jar lid, an old spoon to dig with, and some clean milk cartons.

They began to dig. Hubert pushed the sand around with snorts and sounds. Sylvia daintily filled a carton, turned it upside down and padded the mound silently.

Annie sat back enjoying the sunshine. Rain in the morning, sun in the afternoon. Everything smelled fresh. She looked around at the neat rows of Mr. Sigby's vegetable garden. Peas and beans and corn. The tomatoes were just beginning to ripen. The sun was now shining down brightly. Annie looked up at the house; the back door opened.

"Hubert!" Dorothy called loudly. "Come right in and put on your jacket. You'll catch cold."

Hubert stopped playing. He looked uncertainly from his mother to Annie.

"Hurry up!" his mother said.

He sat still.

"Did you hear me! If you don't come in here right now and put on your jacket, your father will hear about it when we get home!"

Hubert got up hurriedly. He pointed a finger at Annie. "She said I didn't have to."

Dorothy looked with surprise at Annie.

Annie said quickly, "It wasn't very cold so I thought —"

"You should *ask* not *think!*" Dorothy interrupted her.

Annie stood by with her hands at her sides watching Dorothy stick Hubert's hands into his jacket sleeves, and button up all the buttons. Sylvia too.

"There now," Dorothy said lovingly. "That's better!"

Bundled up to his chin, Hubert went back to his play.

"But it's really warm," Annie tried to explain.

Dorothy didn't listen. "Keep your eyes on them," she said sharply.

Dorothy went back into the house. Annie unbuttoned her sweater.

The children sniggered behind their hands and kept sneaking looks at her as if she had done something wrong. Annie pretended not to notice at first. And then as the pokes at each other increased, she felt her face growing red, and grew angry at herself for acting as guilty as they thought she was.

"You're bad!" Hubert said, and threw a cupful of sand in her direction. "My mommy thinks you're bad."

Sylvia looked up then, too. "Bad people go to Hell," she said matter-of-factly. "Grandpa says so."

Annie laughed. It was a hollow forced sound.

"Some people don't believe in Hell," she said, and seeing the look of surprise on Hubert's face, added quickly — "But they're probably wrong. They're probably wrong because —" she couldn't think of a logical reason to give —

"Because Grandpa says so," said Hubert.

"And what Grandpa says is always right," Annie said virtuously.

"That's right," said Hubert.

Mrs. Sigby's face appeared at the kitchen window. She viewed the pleasant scene from inside the frame, and nodded and smiled as she bobbed her head approvingly up and down.

11   Families Are Different

"We're going to have bean soup for dinner," Mrs. Sigby told Annie when Annie came in to set the table.

Annie found herself hesitating, waiting a slight second.

"We always have bean soup on Sundays," Mrs. Sigby said.

Annie nodded and opened the cupboard door.

Dorothy said, "I've gotten out of the habit. Henry never did like bean soup much."

"Well, he should!" Mrs. Sigby's head was shaking up and down vigorously.

Dorothy stopped folding the napkins to look more closely at Annie.

"Your father is a professor, or something like that," she said, not even making it a question.

Annie remembered she had told Mrs. Sigby that her father read a lot. She said hastily — "No, nothing like that. He's in aerodynamics."

A sweet blank look had come over Mrs. Sigby's face. "An engineer is what he is really," Annie added quickly. "Research."

"Then why didn't you say so," said Dorothy, and went back to her napkin folding.

She took each one, folded it lengthwise, then in half, then starting at one corner, rolled it, carefully stuck the end through a napkin ring, fluffed out the vari-pointed tops, and set the napkin ring squarely on the middle of each plate.

They were linen napkins, the real linen kind. Annie found herself hesitating again a little. She glanced at Mrs. Sigby.

"We always use linen napkins for dinner," Mrs. Sigby said.

And Annie went to get the glasses.

They always rinsed each glass and polished it again before setting it on the table, she reminded herself. They always put a butter knife laid crossways above the plate. They didn't use bread and butter plates.

"Put the butter knife *above* each place," Mrs. Sigby called out to her. "We never use bread and butter plates."

Guiltily, Annie started. She had been so anxious to do everything just right that she had gotten ahead of herself.

"It's my mother who is the professor," Annie heard herself saying.

"Your mother!"

"She teaches political science at the Community College."

"My!" said Dorothy, but she didn't sound as if she were much impressed.

"I don't like politics. I never vote without Mr. Sigby's advice," Mrs. Sigby said. "Like Mr. Sigby says — what do women know about voting."

"My mother has classes to teach women about issues and things. They study questions and make reports," Annie said.

"Good heavens, I haven't time enough to take care of my own kids and house, what with all the cooking and cleaning and laundering. Three meals a day — and promptly too. That's one thing Henry has never been able to complain about — meals are always regular at our house!"

Annie recalled, unwillingly, that at her house they sometimes ate TV dinners.

"My husband won't eat TV dinners," Dorothy said proudly, and Annie pretended to be busy shining the glassware.

"Well, some families are not like ours," Mrs. Sigby said, shaking her head as if she felt sorry for all the other families.

"My Henry won't put up with any monkey business, my kids know that! Why once he took off his belt and strapped Hubert where it did the most good for not finishing his dessert."

"He got spanked for not eating *dessert!*" Annie said in amazement.

"It was rhubarb sauce!" Dorothy said sharply.

"Kids should eat what's set before them, that's what Mr. Sigby always says," Mrs. Sigby said.

"That's what Henry says too. Kids grow up the way

their parents teach them! My kids'll grow up knowing who's boss around our house or I'll know the reason why!"

"Most kids nowadays are spoiled rotten. Running around carrying signs and forgetting to cut their hair and put on shoes! I say to Henry — you show me a dirty kid and I can point my finger directly at the guilty party!"

Slowly Annie turned around. Dorothy stood, arm outstretched, pointing directly over Annie's head.

"I saw a piece in the paper the other day," said Mrs. Sigby, "about a boy who told the police he hadn't had a bath for three months!"

"Phew!" said Dorothy.

"What did they do with him?" Annie didn't remember seeing that.

"The judge sentenced him to a shower — and that's all they did with him!" Mrs. Sigby shook her head unbelieving.

"If you ask me, it's his parents they should have jailed. That would have stopped *that* pretty quick."

Annie thought of Awful Jones. She couldn't see how jailing his parents would make any difference in him.

Annie helped get the children ready for dinner, and then helped serve dinner. She jumped up several times to refill the vegetable bowl and put some apple butter on the table when Mrs. Sigby told her to. Nobody said anything.

Sylvia reached across the table and helped herself to a pickle. Her mother reached out and slapped her hand.

"Always ask your mother first," Mr. Sigby said sternly.

"Why can't I have another one?" Sylvia whined.

"Because I said so, that's why!" her mother said.

"Your mother knows best," Mrs. Sigby said sweetly. "Do what she says, and you'll grow up to be a good girl."

"That's right," said Mr. Sigby.

"You're lucky to have such a good mother, isn't she, Annie?" said Mrs. Sigby. "Isn't Sylvia lucky to have such a nice mommy."

Annie looked down at her plate, trying to avoid Dorothy's sharp glance.

"Sit up straight, Hubert," Dorothy said to him. "Sylvia, swallow what you have in your mouth."

Annie sat up very straight, too. She made a point of chewing everything thoroughly and swallowing quickly. She spoke only when spoken to, and said, "Excuse me," every time she left the table to go to the kitchen.

"That's right," Mr. Sigby said once or twice to the children. "Mind your mother."

And Mrs. Sigby added frequently — "Eat all your dinner like good children."

"I want a pickle," Sylvia whined.

Her mother paid no attention.

"A pickle!" Sylvia shouted. "I want a pickle!"

Her mother reached over and slapped again. The spoon the little girl was holding clattered to her plate, and Sylvia began to wail loudly.

"If you don't stop hollering," her mother hollered, "I'm going to lock you in the basement. Stop it! Stop it now — or into the basement you go."

Sylvia looked at her mother and wailed still more loudly.

Her mother moved her chair back threateningly — and the wail squeezed off. Sylvia hiccuped.

"Well, now," said Mrs. Sigby. "That's better! That's a good girl."

"But I want . . ."

"Sylvia! The basement!" — her mother pointed.

Sylvia was quiet.

"You may go with Annie into the kitchen," Dorothy commanded. "But mind you — no more hollering."

Feeling sorry for the little girl, Annie led her into the kitchen. She sat her down on the kitchen stool and gave her the eggbeater to play with.

Sylvia sat happily whirring the thing.

"Now isn't that nice?" Annie asked, and sounded to herself just like Mrs. Sigby.

Sylvia hiccuped. "Bad basement," she chanted to herself. "Bad, very bad basement."

"Oh, the basement's not so bad!" Annie said. "It's really rather nice. I'll take you down there and you'll see — you'll like it!"

Sylvia opened her mouth wide and screamed.

"What's the matter! What's the matter!" Dorothy came rushing into the kitchen, Mrs. Sigby behind her.

Dorothy lifted the big child in her arms. "What did she do to you? Mommie's here, baby, don't you cry!"

"But I didn't do anything," Annie said in earnest puzzlement. "I didn't do anything at all!"

But Sylvia pointed her finger at Annie and cried — "She's going to put me in the basement. She said so!"

Annie gasped. "I did not!"

"Aren't you ashamed," Dorothy said, and clasped Sylvia to her. "Picking on a mere baby!"

"I didn't —" Annie began.

"Did you or did you not mention the basement to Sylvia?"

In consternation Annie looked down at her soapy hands.

"So!" said Dorothy righteously, and carried her child out of the kitchen.

12   Eliot

SLOWLY, Annie finished the dishes and went into the hallway.

Mr. Sigby was in the den with the children. Annie hesitated and looked upstairs. Mrs. Sigby and Dorothy were up there talking. She moved away quickly and stepped into the empty living room.

The shades were still all the way down. She guessed Dorothy wasn't considered company. Annie sat down on one of the chairs. It felt stiff and unwelcoming. She got up and moved to the sofa.

"For heaven's sakes, Annie, what are you doing in there?" Mrs. Sigby stood at the doorway looking at her in surprise.

Annie jumped up. "Nothing," she said.

She followed Mrs. Sigby into the den.

"We are waiting for you, Annie," Mr. Sigby said firmly.

"We always read from the Bible every Sunday," Mrs. Sigby said.

Mr. Sigby began turning the pages of his leather-covered book.

"Sit down, Hubert!" ordered Dorothy. She was holding Sylvia on her lap.

Hastily Hubert sat down, and Annie did too.

Mr. Sigby adjusted his glasses and cleared his throat. "We have been reading about Jacob."

"Hubert and Sylvia know all about Jacob," said Dorothy. "How he bought Esau's birthright for a bowl of pottage, and how he fooled his father into thinking he was Esau and his father blessed him instead."

Annie wondered what a bowl of pottage was. Whatever it was, it didn't sound like much, she thought. For some reason then, she thought of the bean soup Mrs. Sigby had made for their Sunday dinner. She was still hungry, she reflected.

"*. . . and the Lord said to Jacob*": Mr. Sigby was reading slowly. His voice went up and down.

Annie thought of Jacob's trading places with his older brother Esau. She guessed she would have exchanged places with Regina if she could. She had often tried to be like Regina while Regina was gone. Jacob had fooled his father by pretending to be Esau, but she hadn't fooled her father one bit. She had been more like Esau instead of Jacob — giving up what she had for —

"Pottage!" she said out loud. Startled she looked around.

Mr. Sigby raised his head.

"We're way past that!" said Hubert. "Grandpa is telling us about Jacob's fight."

"What fight?"

"With the angel! He met a man and the man fought with him. But the man was really an angel!"

"Why?" said Sylvia.

"Hush!" said Dorothy.

"And Jacob struggled and Jacob strove —" Mr. Sigby did not look back to the page. "And he didn't know who he was fighting or what he was fighting for. All he knew was that he had to keep on fighting. And he got a hold, and held on tight. At last the man cried out, and Jacob let go. 'What is your name?' the man asked. 'My name is Jacob.' 'No,' the man said, 'Your name is now Israel.'"

Sylvia yawned.

Mr. Sigby closed the book. "Then Jacob went forth and became the father of twelve sons and they were called the children of Israel."

"The word of the Lord endureth forever," Mrs. Sigby mumbled, and started suddenly, and opened her eyes wider.

Mrs. Sigby hadn't heard all the story either, thought Annie. She had been sitting there, sleeping with her eyes wide open.

Dorothy hastened the children upstairs to bed and she didn't ask for Annie's help. Mrs. Sigby got up and went into the kitchen. Mr. Sigby switched off the light in the den and turned on the television to a gardening program.

Annie looked around. There was no place for her to go. She opened the front door and went out and sat down on the porch steps. Across the street, the lights were turned on, and the window shades pulled down. She looked into the smooth patch of lawn inside the white fence. No weeds. They weren't "allowed" at the Sigbys'. That was supposed to be funny, Annie told herself, but she didn't feel like laughing.

She hugged her knees and looked at the plastic swan. In the darkness it seemed real. It almost moved. It did move!

"Who's there!" Annie whispered.

A face rose, peering at her. "Annie?"

Annie stood up.

"It's me, Eliot."

"Who?"

The face became part of a body. It was Awful Jones.

"I didn't know your name was Eliot." She giggled.

He grimaced. "I know, it's awful." Then a startled expression came over his face.

She grinned.

"I figured you'd come out sooner or later." He sat down on the step below her. "I've been waiting around. That woman with the kids. How do you stand them?"

"They're just here for a visit. A short visit, I hope." She looked down at his feet. They were bare, and dirty. She wondered how he could walk so far without hurting his feet.

"They toughen up after a while," Awful said.

"Oh," said Annie.

"I haven't worn any shoes for three months. Makes my dad mad. My mom too. They seem to think there's something so terribly important about wearing shoes."

"Some things parents just don't understand," said Annie, automatically.

"They're very insecure," said Awful. "That's their problem."

"Maybe that's it," said Annie.

Awful examined his dirty feet. "My mother thinks taking baths is some sort of religious rite, for gosh sakes."

"My girl friend, Migs, takes a bath every single night. She has to. Her mother says so. Maybe it's because they're Catholic.

"I have a friend who's Catholic who didn't change his socks for two weeks!"

"I guess maybe you wouldn't call him a 'good Catholic,' " Annie said.

"I don't think being Catholic has anything to do with the way you smell," Awful said.

"I guess maybe you're right," said Annie. "Though once Migs' brother tried to kiss me and he really smelled."

Awful looked at her carefully. "Maybe you've got to get used to things like that."

"I'll never get used to the way Migs' brother smells!"

"I meant kissing."

"Oh," Annie said, and thought about it. She had never been kissed by a boy before.

"Migs' mother thought I was terrible. She wouldn't let Robert come over to my house again."

She felt Awful looking at her.

"It's because I'm not Catholic, you know."

Awful said, "My father's not anything. My mother's a little bit of everything, if that's possible. It's not important."

Annie saw the light go on in the hallway. "It is if you're religious."

"Depends on what you mean by *religious*."

"Well, Mr. and Mrs. Sigby are *very* religious. They read the Bible almost every day."

Awful gave a raucous laugh. "Being religious has nothing to do with whether or not you read the Bible any more than with how many baths you take."

Annie stared at him in astonishment.

"You know what I think being religious is?" Awful drew his knees up and stared at the gladiolus against the fence. "I think you have to *like* people to be really religious. Maybe even love them. You've got to look at any person coming up the street and think — he's got as much right to be living as I have."

"That's religion?"

Awful stared at his bare feet intently. "Well, that's what it should be," he said solemnly.

Annie looked at the plastic swan. Then at the white picket fence turning gray in the evening light. She thought of Mrs. Sigby locking the door against a stranger in the neighborhood. She thought of Mr. Sigby calling the police —

"I was somewheres around here the other day," said Awful self-consciously. "Howard told me this is where you'd come to live." He made a face. "Some nutty old guy began shaking a rake at me —"

Annie gasped. "That was Mr. Sigby. He didn't know who you were."

Awful frowned — "And he didn't bother to find out either. He didn't even ask me anything —"

Annie said softly — "Well, you probably wouldn't have answered if he had . . ."

Awful grimaced. "I guess you're right."

He's sort of mixed up, thought Annie, and she felt a little sorry for Awful.

"Here," he said roughly. "I found something for you." He pushed a little wad of fur at her. It mewed.

"A kitten!"

"You can have it," he said offhandedly. "It doesn't belong to anybody."

"A stray?"

"I guess so."

She handed it back to him. "The Sigbys don't like strays. They wouldn't let me keep it."

He tucked it back into his jacket pocket. "That's all right. I'll keep it for you until you go home. You going back home pretty soon?"

She wriggled uncomfortably.

He gave her a brotherly pat on the shoulder. "I guess you're a little mixed up, huh?"

She couldn't help it, she laughed out loud. She had never thought that Awful Jones would be feeling sorry for *her*.

The door behind them flew open.

"Annie!" Mr. Sigby stood there, sharp and questioning.

Annie started guiltily. Awful made a mad scramble, slid off the porch steps, tripped over the plastic swan, picked himself up, and dashed through the gate and down the street.

"Who was that?" Mrs. Sigby came around from behind her husband. "Annie, who was that?"

Annie stood up straight. "A friend," she said.

Mrs. Sigby looked and saw Awful Jones loping around the corner. She gasped. "A friend?" She almost choked.

Annie nodded. "The dirt doesn't matter," she said clearly. "He's very religious. *Really* religious!"

She marched through the door Mr. Sigby was holding open for her.

Dorothy stood in the middle of the hallway, her arms folded. "I could have told you!" she said to her mother. "If you asked me, I could have told you!"

Annie stopped. She faced Dorothy squarely. "You — you *gerbil!*" she shouted.

Mrs. Sigby looked at Annie in bewilderment.

"It's a rodent with a long tail and long hind limbs that leaps!" Annie explained. "The only nice thing about it is it doesn't smell—euphemistically speaking, that is!"

Dorothy's face grew red and she reached out, but Annie dodged and ran up the stairs to her room. She shut the door behind her, and stuck the doorstop in to wedge it closed.

13   The Light in the Closet

ANNIE got into bed without brushing her teeth or washing her face. The Sigbys equated dirt with sin, she thought, feeling pleased with her sinfulness. Being different than they were was a sin to them too. So was forgetfulness, laziness, and not being prompt. The Sigbys liked beans cold and chili without peppers in it, thought weeds were ugly and all children just naturally bad. You squashed kids for asking questions, walloped them for thinking, and bundled them up when it wasn't even cold. The Sigbys acted as if God Himself had given them a private set of rules! Blue dishes on Mondays and only white on Sundays. "Don't think." "Hang up your coat when you come into the house." "The wire hanger — we use the wooden ones for ironing!" Or was it the other way around? Annie sat up in bed, listening.

The Sigbys were going to bed. Mr. Sigby always opened the front door and closed it firmly, snapping the lock securely into place, the last thing before coming upstairs. Mrs. Sigby always went into the bathroom first. Mr. Sigby always mounted the steps after the bathroom door had closed; he always stopped on the third step to look back to make sure he had locked the door, and again on the seventh to put his hand on the railing.

All the lights in the Sigby house were turned off exactly at ten o'clock. No one ever read in bed after ten o'clock. It wasn't allowed.

Annie heard a rap at her door. "Your light is on!" the soft voice accused.

Quickly Annie switched it off, waited a moment or two, and turned it on again. She plopped up her pillows behind her and looked for something to read. Her library book! She had left her library book at home. There was nothing in the room to read but one of Mr. Sigby's Bibles.

It had been sitting there on her dresser ever since the first night she had come. It had been there when she had brought her bag into the room. She had never even bothered to open it. She looked at it, wishing she had remembered to bring her library book.

There was a sudden loud rapping at her door. Mr. Sigby's voice said firmly, "It's after ten o'clock, Annie!" And behind him, Mrs. Sigby reminded — "We always turn the lights off at ten o'clock."

Annie switched off the light and stood in the dark, listening until she had heard the Sigbys go back to bed. Then she quietly and carefully pulled at the dresser, unplugged the lamp, carried the lamp over to her closet, opened the closet door, set the lamp inside, and plugged it to the outlet in that side of the room.

She turned on the lamp so that its light shone only

inside the closet. Pulling the blanket off the bed and a pillow, she stuffed them into her closet too, went in herself and pulled the door closed.

It was rather cozy there with the light on. She crept out once more, took the Bible back in with her and shut the door again.

Pushing aside the shoes and the hems of her dresses, Annie settled herself comfortably and opened the Bible.

In the beginning God created the heaven and the earth . . . And God said: Let there be light. And there was light. And God saw the light, that it was good; and God divided the light from the darkness. And God called the light Day, and the darkness Night. And there was evening and there was morning, one day . . .

It was poetry! thought Annie. She had never known that the Bible was like poetry.

Annie slowly turned the pages, searching. She skipped through the episodes of Noah's Ark and the Tower of Babel, the story of Abraham and of Isaac. When she came to the birth of Esau and Jacob she began to read eagerly.

Finally she reached the part of Jacob, wrestling with the angel by the side of the river. She read it through carefully. "Let me go! Let me go!" she could hear the angel say. But Jacob would not let him go. He knew that he must not let him go. She could hear the angel gasp — "What is your name?" "My name is Jacob," Jacob said. "Your name shall no more be called Jacob, but Israel," the angel told him. "For you have struggled with God and with men and you have prevailed."

Her heart beginning to thump, Annie read that again . . . "and you have prevailed." What did it mean? Something tremendous had happened to Jacob. What was it?

She leaned back, thinking about it, and her elbow pressed into one of her shoes. Annie turned off the light, pushed open the closet door and dragged the bedding back to her bed.

Just as she fell asleep, she thought she saw it. She saw its meaning fleetingly, but exactly. But when she awoke in the morning, it was gone. It was almost as if it had just slipped away from her. It had fallen over the edge of the bed, she thought sleepily. She even heard the sound it made falling, and opening her eyes, she made a grab for it.

"Annie!" Mrs. Sigby's scolding tone came to her. There was another firm knock on the door. "We are all waiting for you, Annie!"

Annie jumped out of bed. It was already eight-thirty. She was late for breakfast. Now she had broken the most important rule of all!

14 "Call Me Jacob"

Aɴɴɪᴇ left her bag outside the door, and turned the knob quietly.

They were all there. Annie closed the door behind her.

"I'm home," she said, looking into the living room. No one even noticed.

"I'm home," she said a little louder.

Her father was slumped in his chair, curling his toes in his stocking feet. Her mother turned.

"Annie!" said Regina.

Annie had forgotten how tall Regina was—taller than her mother. Annie's nose was pressed into Regina's shoulder with the force of the hug.

Annie looked around quickly. There was no black African sitting on their sofa. Annie guessed Regina had changed her mind, and for some reason, she felt a little disappointed.

"Annie's home!" said Regina.

Her father looked at Annie briefly. He said to Regina — "You can tell her she might as well stay for dinner. That is if she can bear to put up with us that long."

Annie gulped. Her father was still not speaking to her!

"Oh for heaven's sakes!" said Regina, and threw her hands into the air. "Yesterday I found a kid upstairs who won't talk to adults and today there's an adult downstairs who won't talk to kids!"

Mrs. Lee laughed. She laughed in that hearty big voice of hers. Grinning sourly, Mr. Lee lowered his book.

Annie carried her bag up to her room. She looked in through Howard's open door.

He was sitting cross-legged on his bed, his record player was on, wheezing a thin stream of music faintly. An odd smell hung over the room. Annie sniffed.

"Is something burning or something?" She glanced around the room.

"Sure!" he said. "How do you like it?"

"It stinks!"

Howard sniffed deeply. "It's supposed to! It's incense. All you have to do is light it first thing in the morning and it keeps burning all day."

"You mean you're going to let that stuff burn up here all day?"

"Mom won't let me burn it in the living room," he said as if he couldn't understand it.

Annie held her nose elaborately with the fingertips of one hand, and batted the air with the other. "Thank goodness!"

"Well, if you don't like it, you can go back to the Sigbys!" he yelled after her.

"Maybe I will!" she shouted back at him, but there was no conviction in her voice.

Annie went on into her own room; Regina came up the stairs and into Annie's room too.

"Maybe you can tell me what's going on here," Regina suggested, and plopped down on Annie's bed.

"Nothing's going on," Annie said. "Nothing more than usual." There was a scratchy feeling in her throat. She thought of how she had unceremoniously left the Sigbys, not even eating breakfast. Suddenly her hollowness reached all the way down to her knees. She sat down quickly. Her father didn't want her to come home!

"What's all this about your running away?"

"I didn't run away!"

"Didn't you?"

"Well, yes."

Regina stopped peering at her and went to the chest of drawers. She fidgeted with the things on the top and examined something on her chin.

"Once I ran away," she said.

"You?" Her surprise surprised even Regina. Regina turned around to face her.

"I was older than you," she said. "I ran away from school."

"Oh, school," Annie said.

"I thought there wasn't anything they could teach *me* — not the way I wanted to learn it."

"What happened?"

"Nothing happened. That was the trouble. I didn't

learn anything — worth learning that is. And so I went back. I lost a whole quarter—that's learning the hard way, I guess."

"Is there an easy way?" Annie looked at herself in the mirror.

"Not when you are your father's daughter."

Annie sighed. "Well, I'm not," she said.

"Not what?" Regina said as if Annie had changed the subject.

"Not like father. Not like him at all."

Regina swung about impatiently. "You," she said, "are stubborn, exasperating, and utterly impossible! No one can tell you anything!"

"That's father you're talking about!" said Annie hotly. "Not me!"

"That's just what I've been saying!" shouted Regina. "You're just exactly like him!"

Annie stared at her.

"They're in there yelling at each other!" Howard shouted down the stairs.

Their mother's voice floated up to them — she must have been talking out the back door to a neighbor. "It's nice to have everybody back home!" she said.

Annie laughed. It had never seemed funny to her before, but it did now. Her mother was always happiest in the middle of commotion. She liked people to speak up, to argue when they disagreed, and to shout if it made them feel better. She liked people to say what they meant. Her father was the quieter one — like she was . . . "Oh!" And she looked quickly at Regina.

"I'm not a bit like that," Annie protested weakly.

Regina turned around slowly. She let her eyes travel around the room — the books and the magazines and the papers. The clippings on the walls, the sharpened pencils . . . She made a funny little face when her glance rested on the suitcase Annie had dumped on the bed.

"When he was just a kid he ran away from home too. You know why?"

Annie shook her head.

"He wanted to join the army and fight. He didn't know what he was fighting for, or why — he just knew he had to fight . . ."

Annie listened. Regina's voice seemed to echo another in the back corners of her mind. She heard Mr. Sigby's voice — "and Jacob struggled and Jacob strove. And he didn't know who he was fighting or what he was fighting for — but he knew he had to keep on fighting."

"Jacob," she whispered. "Jacob and the angel."

Regina hardly heard her. "After he got home he knew he had really been fighting only himself."

Annie took a deep breath. "I know! I know!"

"I guess it's something you have to go through — in order to grow up," Regina said.

"Like Jacob!" said Annie clearly, though she was not really talking to Regina. "You have to *prevail!*"

Regina looked at her uncomprehendingly. The sound of Howard discussing something at the top of his voice came to them.

"We'd better go down," said Regina eagerly.

Slowly Annie followed after her. Regina liked noise and confusion too.

"What's the matter now?" Annie heard Regina say as she burst into the living room.

Annie came in time to see her mother raise her eyebrows, and give a helpless little smile. Her father was standing regarding them all owlishly.

"I'll tell you what's the matter!" He waved his arms to include them all.

"What?" said Regina calmly.

But he looked as if he didn't know quite where to begin. "Gerbils!" he said suddenly. "Yesterday the gerbils were running all around my bedroom!"

"I thought you sold them," Annie said to Howard.

"Nah," said Howard. "She chickened out."

"This morning," their father continued, "there was that strange kid in the bathroom."

"Awful!" said Annie, wondering where he was now. She thought about him and the little stray kitten he was keeping for her.

"It is, isn't it?" said Regina.

"Today I called the furnace people about the strange burning smell — " he looked accusingly at Mrs. Lee.

"Incense," she said helplessly.

"My son," he went right on, "sits half the day with his arms folded and his legs crossed staring at the ceiling."

"I was contemplating!" said Howard with an injured air. "Like the Buddhists do!"

His father continued — "My oldest daughter traipses

all over Europe preferring to study every culture but her own . . ."

Regina said, "Well, I already have two degrees!"

"And my younger daughter leaves home to live somewhere else . . ."

"I'm back!" said Annie.

Her father asked — "Has everyone gone crazy?"

Annie shifted from one foot to the other and looked at Howard. Howard crossed his arms and searched for an answer on the ceiling.

"I don't think you have any call to complain about us doing exactly what you taught us to do," Regina said.

Her father looked at her in amazement. "*I* taught you to hitchhike, and burn incense, and go to find other families to live with!"

"Think!" said Regina.

"Yeah," said Howard. "That's what you're always telling us to do."

Regina said firmly — "Why blame us for not doing exactly what *you* think we should do — when you taught us to think for ourselves."

Their father opened his mouth and nothing came out.

"Let's all go in and have some lunch," their mother said quickly, brightly.

And suddenly their father laughed.

They had baloney sandwiches for lunch, sitting around the kitchen table together. They were using linen napkins.

"I forgot to get paper ones," Mrs. Lee said matter-of-factly.

"Well, no one's perfect," Annie said.

Regina's laugh bounced out.

"Annie, Annie — " her mother said with a loud happy sigh.

"Call me Jacob," Annie said, and looking around at the baffled faces of her family, she grinned.